To AMY

DOCTOR TRIPPS
KAIJU COCKTAIL

THE MONSTERS
GOT BIG

DOCTOR TRIPPS
KAIJU COCKTAIL

KIT COX

Published by Telos Moonrise (an imprint of
Telos Publishing) 17 Pendre Avenue, Prestatyn,
Denbighshire, LL19 9SH

Doctor Tripps: Kaiju Cocktail © 2013 Kit Cox

ISBN: 978-1-84583-867-6

British Library Cataloguing in Publication Data. A
catalogue record for this book is available from the
British Library.

DEDICATED TO
Amber & Connor

1
STEAMED

The applause moved around the room like a rolling tide as Dr Horatio Tripps pulled on his coat and hurried to the door. He was angry. It was not an ovation for his departure, however, but an expression of admiration from his fellow onlookers for the machine that now stood rumbling in the middle of the auditorium. Excited scientists and journalists pushed forward to see its flywheels spin and its belts turn, as a thick cloud of blackness curled upward into the miasma of pipe and cigar smoke that hung in the rafters, before curling and heading out through an open window into the cold, grey London air. A fact that was a source of some consternation for Tripps.

As Tripps passed through the huge entrance lobby of the Royal Society buildings, statues of some of the greatest names in science looked down upon him with blank eyes.

Tripps was a tall man, dressed in some of London's finest tailored fabrics. His coat was a light beige with all the trimmings picked out in dark maroon piping, his trousers were pinstriped with the same colours and his deep black boots were so highly polished that you could see the whole world darkly reflected in them.

A stocky porter hailed a carriage for the departing gentleman, trying hard not to look at the face of the man beside him, who fussed at a pair of black suede gloves. Tripps did not observe the man's uncomfortable stance; in fact he rarely noticed anyone look away from him anymore. Other people's opinions no longer mattered when he had so much important work still to do.

He had a noble face, some would even say royal, with a striking profile featuring a well defined Roman nose, immaculately preened, silver-grey handlebar moustache and square jaw. He kept his eyes covered with a pair of glasses with round, obsidian lenses that fit so snugly they appeared to be part of his face, and hid any emotion that may otherwise display.

It was however his cranium that caused discomfort in others, for it had been replaced with a glass dome that clearly displayed his brain. It was the ultimate accessory for the vainest of intellectuals. It was the art of craniectomy taken to its farthest point.

With his gloves now on, the doctor pulled from his pocket a folded hat-brim that he slid effortlessly over the dome, giving it the look of a bizarre bowler hat. A further dip into his pocket and he dropped some coins into the porter's outstretched hand and boarded the carriage.

The livery was that of the fine cabs of the great City of the Empire, all bottle green panelling and gold edging. The driver sat on his platform, not nursing patient horses but instead cradling the many levers of a fine, polished brass, steam powered traction engine that propelled them forward.

As they drove, Tripps watched the white-grey smoke from his hired carriage curl up into the air and briefly tangle with the thick black cloud still emanating from the grand window of the society room in which the demonstration continued. In the smoke, he perceived two great monsters entwined in fight, the White Dragon of Albion, its eyes the colour of Industry, chest full and heaving with proud thoughts of Empire while it's monumental wings cast all into shadow. And then he saw the Black Dragon of Europe, bitter, twisted and dirty, snapping at Albion's heels.

The carriage sped on over rough cobbled streets while grubby-faced youngsters ran for cover, and the honest folk who still favoured the horse tried to calm their skittish charges from the noise of the machine as it passed.

Some houses still displayed the remnants of black flags and bunting, tokens of an Empire that still mourned the passing of a great Queen and Empress. Other establishments had moved on, and were now sparkling from a lick of new paint and optimistic thoughts of a glorious future under the reign of a new King.

Finally they arrived at the Limehouse docks and the impressive sculpted glass domicile and laboratory of the doctor. It clung to the dockside like a magnificent crystal turtle, come out from the surf to lay its twisted inventions, like eggs, in the grime of London town.

Tripps flung himself from the cab so hard that his iron-shod heels sparked off the cobbles. Turning quickly, he handed many paper notes to the surprised and happy driver before stalking inside his home, his mind on fire with hatred and ideas.

The woman who greeted him glided almost

silently across the floor. Her skin was pale and had a shine to it that gave the impression that her fine features had been carved from a pearl. Her hair was piled on her head and sculpted to resemble an octopus; the hair-clips were strange and alien eyes, while eight braids hung down around her face, back-curled with wire to finish the topiary, giving an altogether unsettling look.

When she saw the doctor's face, inflamed with anger, her hair turned suddenly from a soft, silky orange to a dark, stormy blue. Tripps handed her his coat, gloves and hat-brim.

'He was German, you could hear it in every vowel,' he said in a deep, educated voice.

Then he walked past the woman and disappeared into his laboratory without another word.

The woman turned flawlessly on the spot, and her long dress, decorated with a myriad of tiny scales, caught the fading light and shone dreams of the sea across the walls. She hung up the doctor's outer garments besides a row of other finely-tailored jackets in many colours, all with matching accessories, and followed him soundlessly in her quiet glide, the double doors opening with a silent swish before her.

The laboratory beyond was vast and spacious, having more in common with the greenhouses of Kew than with the stuffy rooms of Burlington House, where other learned men practiced their craft. Every inch was occupied either with a workbench, piled high with intricate apparatus and wonderful nameless machines, or instead was filled with a huge and exotic plant or tree, many with strange colourful blooms. Sweet and heavy fragrances filled the air.

Sat in a well-stuffed, red leather captain's chair at the room's centre was the doctor. He was looking out of the expansive window at the dock and the huge, newly constructed, ark-like ship, the *Arc*, that was moored there.

'Bring me a large gin,' he said without ceremony. 'I need to think.'

The delicate woman picked up a small bell and rang it twice. All was quiet. The doctor sat, obsidian eyes on the vessel before him; the woman waited, her hair changing to a lighter blue, the braids moving slightly as if restless. Then there was movement in the lab. The tall ferns shifted and what must have once been one of the ape family shuffled from the vegetation. The creature was dressed in the manner of a butler, but it had the head of a common housefly grown to a size to match its simian body. Through the jacket, a hole had been neatly cut from which wings protruded and occasionally buzzed, although they were far too small to lift the primate's bulk.

It approached with a silver tray held tightly in one of its strong hands, upon it a large black medicine bottle and a crystal glass goblet, both of which were reflected back multiple times in the butler's compound eyes.

The creature passed the woman, who scowled slightly at its presence, and reached the chair with agile grace. Taking the bottle, it filled the glass with gin and placed it into the doctor's open hand.

'Thank you, Flyn,' said the doctor, and he drank deeply of the juniper spirit that eased his thoughts and relaxed his mind. The fly/monkey hybrid, task complete, moved back into the foliage, and once again the room fell quiet.

Darkness had fallen when the doctor rose to his feet.

'Igor, we need to pack!' he exclaimed, and the

woman's eyes shot open.

She was still stood where she had been upon entering the room, but her hair was now a rich orange.

'What shall I pack, sir?' she asked. Her voice was gentle and had a melody to it that sounded like singing.

'Everything!' Tripps continued excitedly. 'It's time we made changes; to ensure everything stays the same.'

At this, a big smile crossed both Tripps' and Igor's faces. The woman was so happy to be finally escaping the claustrophobic, dirty streets of London and moving on to the world she had been promised so many years before.

'Will we be taking Flyn and the LUMPs, sir, or shall I administer the serum?' she asked with a sparkle of malicious glee.

'Oh, most certainly, we will be taking everyone. We have things to do and we can't do them here; people would stop us. Flyn can continue to keep house and the LUMPs can build. It will be dangerous work, but what we lose we can replace.' The doctor looked at Igor. 'And you, my beautiful creature of the seas, can help me in my work. We will be gone a few years, but when we return we will be ready for war.'

Igor could contain herself no longer and clapped her hands together in joy. Between her fingers was a delicate webbing of skin, decorated with small swirls of colour, which pulsed in time with her clapping hands.

Later that night, a constant line of small, chattering shapes passed strange objects from the doctor's laboratory and house out to the large wooden ship that rocked gently in its moorings. As the first rays of light crept up the Thames, the magnificent vessel was at last fully loaded, moored on two parallel jetties. Above it, tethered by huge ropes, hovered a vast, blimp-like balloon that strained for the heavens.

On deck stood the doctor, resplendent in a fine tailed frock coat of emerald velvet. Beside him was the beautiful Igor dressed in a nautical jacket and floor-length dress, the colour of a Caribbean sea. Behind them both, the squat hairy shape of Flyn the butler ushered an uncountable number of small, chattering, winged monkeys below deck. They jostled like children, all trying to be the last to go below and away from the rising sun, the warmth of which they craved to feel on their fur.

Once the last of the LUMPs had descended, the doctor moved to the ship's prow and addressed the large crowd of dockworkers that had gathered while passing on their way to work, drawn by the first light of dawn and distracted on their way by the mighty tethered balloon atop this impressive craft.

'Goodbye, London,' the doctor orated. 'We do not leave you in your hour of need. We merely retire like the great King Arthur to a place of safety and will return when you need us most. Try not to get too distracted by progress while we are gone.'

And with that, Tripps pulled a lever, the ropes securing the vessel broke free with an ear splitting crack and the ship sailed quickly up into the clouds while tiny hairy faces peered from every porthole.

The crowd watched it go and then as one turned toward the now abandoned building; it sparkled like an open treasure chest in the morning rays, unguarded and inviting.

'Got to be something good inside there?' a gruff voice said from the throng of people.

'He may have been a loony but he was a rich loony,' said a slightly lighter voice, with a Scottish brogue.

There was the briefest of pauses before the crowd surged for the door, all eyes now turned away from the clouds and the departing wonder that had drawn them all here. This was a shame, because if anyone of them had looked up, they might have seen the queer-shaped metal ball falling down at quite some speed towards them.

As the crowd went in the front door, the ball smashed in through the roof, and in a blinding white flash, most of Limehouse docks disappeared.

2
DIESEL

Twelve Years Later

It was a cool September evening, almost 12 years after the explosion that rocked Limehouse docks and started a series of regeneration projects for the area.

Rudolph Diesel had led a good life. It had admittedly been filled with trauma, but then again, who hasn't seen a few upsets in their time? He was a citizen of the world; French born but brought up as a German by his parents, who chose to live in England, a situation he most certainly appreciated.

So, him being a man of the world, it wasn't a surprise that he could see war hovering so close. He took nearly every newspaper in the languages he could read, and already everyone was pointing fingers at everyone else, but Diesel bore no clear allegiances to any of them to be able to express his concerns.

All it would take was one little nudge, and then where would it all go? Who would be the quiet voice of reason, when everyone started shouting? It was thoughts like this that had guided Diesel throughout his entire life.

When as a young man he had survived typhoid, he'd vowed he didn't want anyone to go through the suffering he had, but as he wasn't a doctor he couldn't develop a breakthrough cure, despite reading many books.

Diesel had studied as an engineer and made great advances in the mechanics of refrigeration, thinking of its potential use for others in helping keep food fresh and stopping the spread of disease, before a steam engine had almost taken his life.

After the accident, however, he realised he could do something to move folk away from the dangers of exploding steam-powered machines or devices, and with this in mind had designed and built the first diesel engine.

That's when it had all started. The world had taken this technology to its collective heart, and Diesel was the future.

Then, about ten years ago, the letters had started to arrive. All were handwritten and all were delivered to the upper rooms of his house. He had never seen anyone enter or climb his property, but they kept coming, with increasing frequency. Sometimes one would be left on his balcony, the one that overlooked the centre of Berlin. Often he would find one on his bedside table or on the bedroom floor. More than once they were found pushed into the putty of the window frame … on the outside of the building!

The letters were never truly threatening. They were often just factual. But they would talk of a world ruined by weapons of war powered by diesel engines, a dark future of machines able to carry on spouting out dirt and muck to taint the clouds, as they tore up the planet.

Diesel had wished he couldn't see the truth in the letters, all of which were signed by the mysterious Dr Tripps, but he knew that the future they spoke of was probable and the only way to halt it was to fight it and find a solution, as he had always strived to do. So he had gathered together in secret like-minded scientists who had no true home country, no patriotic allegiance, and they had made plans.

They built a vast factory, an industrious building on legs, a place that could survive with very little manpower, even in the harshest regions of the world.

This factory would be able to create some of the greatest machines, and all were to be made for the forces of good. There were vast diesel titans ready to fight any vehicle a country used for war; they would all be emblazoned with the badge of Athena, to prove they were on the side of right, with wisdom in all their motives.

Diesel smiled. The birthplace of these machines of peace would soon be under his feet, because he was on a boat travelling across the English Channel, and the Diesel factory was hunkered deep below on the sea floor, waiting. But there would be a price for creating these works. The first titan to rise would give him away, endangering the family he could not bring with him. Thus, he was to fake his own death.

Before leaving port he had given his personal belongings to impoverished yet honest fisherman, along with vast amounts of money. They would wait for a while, then produce them as proof that they had found him dead, his body too ravaged by the sea to bring home. So here he stood on the stern of the *SS*

Dresden, looking down into the cold waters beneath him, waiting to see the sign.

Diesel cast his mind back to the last letter he had received. It had been the strangest yet and, as he stood waiting, he took it once again from his pocket and read.

Rudolph the Destroyer,

Your dark future is almost upon us.
Supported by your dirty engines, the powers of the world wait either side of a thin red line.
They will become monsters. I have foreseen this and I will protect you all.
To fight fire you must use fire. To fight monsters you must use monsters.
First I will prevent. Then I will return the world back to a simpler time of steam.
You have been warned and saved.
Do not try to stop me.

Dr Tripps.

There it was, deep under the water, a light cutting through the murk. Checking no-one was around to see, Diesel removed his coat and revealed the diving suit underneath. He folded the coat neatly onto the deck and jumped into the water with the smallest of splashes.

The cold water took his breath away, but he feared someone would see him, so, although he was an elderly man, he quickly took a deep breath and dived beneath the waves. Cold filled his very soul for a few moments and then he was aware of the craft beneath him and other hands guiding him forward and into a water-filled room.

Hatches were sealed, and slowly the water drained away. Diesel found himself in a small room with one other person: a man he knew and trusted. He was possibly older than Diesel but as a retired soldier he was physically fitter and healthier-looking.

Well, in certain aspects maybe not so. The soldier had lost a hand at some stage. Diesel had recently replaced it with an apparatus of his own design. And a burn had disfigured some of the soldier's face.

The man had known Diesel for many years and had become a good friend. He was more than happy to hide out with Diesel's crew for the rest of his days under the sea. He felt he owed a lot to Diesel and had sworn to protect him. The soldier opened the hatch, and together Diesel and his friend entered the bridge of the submarine that was already on its way to Diesel Base One.

The vast dome of Diesel Base One – DB1 for short – was being claimed by the sea. Barnacles had started to encrust its rust-red surface and seaweed had anchored itself around every warm water vent. It had already looked something like a vast mechanical crab when it had entered the surf several years earlier, its huge dome supported high on six giant hydraulic legs, but now it truly resembled some prehistoric brooding crustacean, lurking at the bottom of the sea.

Inside, scientists and mechanics were working on the Earth's defence, monitoring every radio station for any news of aggression that needed to be crushed, all under the attentive supervision of Diesel's Head of Security.

Unfortunately for them, the man they needed to be listening out for didn't use the radio. He didn't need to, as everyone he wanted was within bell-ringing distance.

Dr Tripps had not been idle over the years. He had built a base in the volcanic clouds above Hawaii while recruiting an army of followers on the ground who were working hard on his vision of saving the world from Diesel and effecting a return to steam.

This was the moment of his greatest creation. A liquid distilled from the very air itself, a vivid, translucent green that glowed with an inner light. He mixed it with other concoctions and experimented on the LUMPs, cataloguing the various results, with Igor ever present, ready to administer the serum should anything get out of hand.

Happy with the conclusions, he sent bottles to his agents around the world. 'The Steamers' they called themselves, and they all had the same instructions: to somehow get the cocktail into the system, however they saw fit.

Some chose to pour the strange liquid into the drinking water of a town, reliably informed it would not dilute but instead wait in large drops ready to infect the unwary. Others chose to secrete it amongst bottles of pop, hoping a large dose in one place could do more damage. Yet more of the agents fed it to crops or animals, expecting to infect the food chain. In all honesty it did not matter what they did, as Dr Tripps' Kaiju Cocktail was designed for all environments, all animals, and all humans.

Tripps loved the word 'Kaiju'; it was ancient in

its linguistic history, yet it sounded alien to European ears. It was Japanese for 'strange beast', and he was planning on creating the strangest beasts the world had ever seen ... and the best thing of all was that Dr Tripps would be able to control each and every one of them.

3
SHEEPZILLA

The creature awoke in a field.

It knew straight away that something had changed. It could vaguely remember being ushered down a road, with a flock of its own kind, all jostling for space. It thought this might have been earlier that morning, but it wasn't sure. It remembered the sweet taste of the green grass in the new meadow and it also remembered the two-legs with the bottle.

The two-legs had approached, pouring something from the bottle onto the grass in front of it. The liquid had made the grass taste even sweeter, and reminded its body of when it had been newly born, frolicking in the fields, bouncing as high as its new legs would lift it. Now it just felt dazed and heavy. The familiar bleat of its companions was absent and it cast its eyes about looking for any predator that might be responsible for the lack of sound.

The rest of the animals were huddled together in the top corner of the paddock and the creature feared the worst. It realised that it was the victim; the heavy weight meant it had already been pinned and soon would meet its end in the jaws of a wolf or bear. It tried to stand, to escape, and was surprised to find that it was able to do so with ease. But it felt strange. Even when it was up on four legs it wanted to rise higher still, to stand on its hind legs – which felt so much stronger now – and take the weight off its forelegs that seemed more adapted to another purpose.

It pushed on up, and soon it could see above the trees and down into the valley. Pains shot through its stomach as if the two-legs had kept it in the barn too long and failed to fill the steel troughs with pellets. It truly was a monstrous hunger. It looked down at the treetops covered with rich green leaves and snapped up a couple of bites, branches and all. It began chewing happily.

But before long it started to crave more than the vegetation. It looked about, and then bent down into the corner of the paddock and started chomping on its little woollen companions until its mouth was hot and the field was full of panicked bleating.

A shout of dismay attracted it and there, by the gate, stood the two-legs with its stick and trained wolves. They all cowered before it, and although its wool was already red and its stomach full, it couldn't resist finding out what these other creatures tasted like.

The wolves had moved oh so very fast, but the two-legs had tasted better than grass, and the creature remembered where there had been many more. As it ran its large pink tongue around its huge teeth, pushing the two-legs' stick from between them, it watched a large metal snake coming up the valley. The creature had watched it many times going away, sometimes with sections of it full of worried bleating. It remembered the covered parts of it, full of windows, the faces of so many two-legs looking out at it as it minded its own business in its field.

It had often wondered where they were all going in such a hurry. It seemed a shame not to at least see if it could catch up and try more of them; it was, after all, feeling hungry again.

The Arch Duke was not entirely happy with the meal that had been placed before him in the overly lavish buffet car, but then again he had never truly been a fan of eating on the move. It didn't feel right to be feasting while the scenery changed with such a blur, and it was because of this that he closed the blinds. Lost in the now-shuttered room, he felt his appetite return and decided on the lamb shank rather than the chicken dish. His stomach rumbled in full approval.

The policeman in the adjoining carriage was glad of the moving scenery. He had a chicken leg for his lunch that had been given to him by the train's chef as he passed. It was going to be a long day after they alighted at Sarajevo station and he was certainly happy to get a bite to eat now, as he was fairly sure no-one would think to feed him during the day. He took a bite of the poultry and looked out at the rolling hills.

What he saw stumbling awkwardly toward them made him choke on his last ever meal.

The creature must have been 30 feet tall, walking on powerful hind legs, their flesh dark as pitch. The body was a wiry mass of pale cream, woollen curls, tinged red around the chest, and it had two twisted black arms held awkwardly before it, as if it had not quite become accustomed to their worth. The fingers of the large, claw-like hands twitched in the air as they swung from the outstretched limbs.

The creature's head was long and dark, with huge, bulging eyes spinning this way and that, as if struggling to focus. It's pink tongue lolled out over crooked tombstone teeth and red gore dripped from its mouth, adding to the stain down its front.

The policeman took his cue and ran for the Arch Duke's dining carriage, shouting the alarm to his colleagues as he did so. His shocked presence amongst the diners was instant cause for alarm. Faces turned to the stammering man, who just pointed toward the windows with fear etched across his features. The politician, not wanting to seem alarmed, simply turned and raised the blind beside him. The last thing he saw was a huge, gnarled black hand before the carriage was crushed beyond recognition.

Those men who had heeded their fellow officer's warning had taken to their feet, weapons drawn against possible attackers, when the carriage they were in tilted alarmingly and rose into the sky. Even the most sure-footed man was thrown from his feet as the compartment went from the horizontal to the vertical. It was only the seats that kept them all from ending in a heap, as loose travel chests flew down to meet some of them in a bone-crunching halt.

A snapping sound reverberated through the train and suddenly the carriage fell to impact on its end, before wobbling and slowly toppling onto its roof. Something collided with it again and it spun through 180 degrees before coming to a halt against another felled carriage.

'Noooo!' shouted the doctor, far above in the clouds. 'The train was steam-driven. It's destroying the wrong things.'

Tripps had bolted onto his own glass cranium an apparatus that spun and buzzed with clockwork parts and tubes of green cocktail. He threw his hands in the air, and miles below, the titanic sheep creature did the same. The only difference was the doctor's action didn't throw the twisted frame of a railway carriage high above his head.

The creature, its actions partly its own but now mostly those of the crazed doctor, put its giant head in its hands, ignoring the uniformed men who swarmed from the many sections of the wrecked train.

It soon turned its maddened eyes on them when rifles started to crack and it felt the whizz of bullets thudding into its soft flesh. It let out a loud 'Baaaaa' that seemed to stop the tiny two-legs in their tracks, however it was at this precise moment that the thrown train carriage came back down and thudded hard into the sheep monster's head.

For a second it stood there, wearing the carriage like a hat. The impact had driven about a quarter of the dining car into its brain, and it let out a very quiet and confused bleat before tipping forward onto the train beneath it with a crash that moved the ground.

'Blast it!' shouted the doctor, tearing the apparatus from his head and letting it swing away on its extended cables, which instantly disappeared into the ceiling with a whirr. 'What kind of moron uses a sheep as a base for one of my monsters?'

Igor was stood before a large table full of levers and dials. Her hair turned ruby red and she reached out to one of the larger controls, disengaging its break and sliding it down, before gliding over to the doctor.

'It will be gone soon,' she sang in her gentle tones, 'and then we can have another go somewhere else. This was only a practice, remember. I doubt the loss of one train will have much impact on the world.'

Far below, the policemen, and those passengers that could, were running. It seemed that in 12 years the common man had been slowly learning his lessons, and the glowing ball descending from the sky seemed like an important tutorial.

Unfortunately the lesson they needed to learn wasn't just to run quicker. And so, in the fields just outside Sarajevo, a large section of countryside disappeared in a blinding flash of white light. It took with it a fair amount of railway line, several police, a giant sheep monster, and Arch Duke Franz Ferdinand and his family.

4
SOCIETIES

Somewhere deep in the Sussex countryside, a phone rang. Two men looked up from beneath the bonnet of a big green automobile, parked in front of an impressive manor house, and looked about them. The elder of the two men was dressed in tweeds and sported a beard you could hide a circus midget in. The younger was dressed in overalls and had the kind of handsome face you only find in one in every hundred farm workers.

'What the dickens is that?' uttered the elder man, never a big enthusiast of things out of his normal routine. 'I believe it's your telephone sir. Lady Em had it installed last month,' said the lad, with a trained inflection to his voice that hid any of the frustrations of explaining something for the hundredth time; a skill found in most below-stairs staff when talking to their employers.

'What the dash did she do that for?'

'I believe it was after you told her she could call you at any time she needed help and you'd come running.'

There was a long pause as the bell continued to ring somewhere in the house.

'We best go answer it then,' said the bearded gentleman, suddenly happy with its intrusion into his routine.

A little while later, the Lord and his young charge were standing by the ringing device.

'Well, answer it then. You youngsters have a knack for this kind of thing,' the Lord said with a friendly if somewhat patronising wink.

The lad bent forward and picked up the handset, putting it close to his ear. 'Ahoy Ahoy!' he said with a proud smile, on remembering the correct way to answer the device.

'Lord Branding?' a crackly voice said.

'I'll just get him for you. Who can I say is calling?'

Already the Lord was retreating and waving his hands about to show he wanted nothing to do with the thing. If it wasn't the statuesque Lady Em, he certainly didn't feel like going running to aid anybody else.

'It's the Order,' said the voice.

The lad put his hand over the mouthpiece and almost hissed at his employer, who was still backing away.

'It's the Order. You can't ignore it.'

'I dashed well can. They haven't been in touch for 13 years, and I've found all those years rather lucky, despite appearances, and not died in one of them.'

A boast the Lord was very proud of considering his family's track record when it came to exploring the Empire, or for that matter exploring the local village.

'You can't ignore them. They send people,' the lad said, his eyes growing wide, having heard all the stories about them from his benefactor.

The two men looked at each other for a while before a decision was made.

'How old are you now, Iron?' said the Lord, a twinkle returning to his eye.

'I'm almost 16, sir.'

In fact it was less than a month to the boy's birthday. He'd been dropping hints to anyone who would listen about ideas for presents. He'd always liked playing knights as a child, hunting dragons and righting wrongs. He even had the wooden sword and knitted chain-mail armour to prove it; but he was now rather hoping for a rifle to hunt partridge with, as a sign of his maturity.

'Well then you're almost a grown man. You take the call and pretend you're me.'

'What … I can't do that, this is *the Order*! They would know.'

A distant 'Hello, hello?' could be heard from the handset.

Iron, his face going from scared, to cross, to resigned, placed the receiver back against his ear. At the very least it might put him in good running for the rifle.

'Lord Branding here. Dash it, what do you want, man? I was in the middle of a ham supper.'

'I don't sound like that!' the Lord blustered.

Iron slammed his hand back over the mouthpiece.

'Then you take the call!'

He wasn't surprised to see Lord Branding wave the receiver back towards him with a mumbled, 'Carry on …'

The voice on the phone continued, '… so we're calling in agents and sending them back out into the field. Seems we were wrong, there are monsters out there still, and the blighters have gotten big.'

'Erm … Yes, big, back in the field,' Iron stammered with a level of confusion.

'So you're back in then?'

'Of course I'm back in.' Iron pushed out his chest, glancing across at Lord Branding with a happy smile, a smile that soon faded when he saw the Lord's face. He barely registered as the voice at the other end of the phone announced it would send round documents and equipment and with a cheery 'Toodle pip!' was gone.

Iron replaced the receiver.

'What? What's the matter?' asked Iron, seeing Lord Branding's pale demeanour.

The Lord said something, so quietly whispered it couldn't be heard, even in the silent room.

'Sorry, I didn't catch that,' said Iron, leaning in.

Again the Lord whispered, but with a little more power to his voice this time. 'I've never said "yes". I just pay my membership, get my secret ring and hope history will remember me as one of the heroes of the old Empire.' The room was so quiet you could hear a revelation drop. 'They don't even know what I look like. I avoided the club in case I accidentally got roped in.'

He looked at Iron as if seeing him for the first time, then the corners of his mouth twitched.

'They don't know what I look like!' he said a little louder, his face pulling into a smile as he slapped his hands onto Iron's shoulders. 'They don't know what I look like!' he said again, with all the power of a man in church who's just found out he hasn't been sinning.

Iron's face fell.

'No, you can't mean …'

'Of course I do. You're young. You're handsome. You're expendable. And besides, *you* said yes, I didn't. And the Order always knows.'

Iron fell back into a chair, the weight of the situation hitting him full force.

'Oh crikey. I've become a Dragon.'

The rain lashed the streets of London and filled the gutters with torrents of water. Every raindrop seemed to wash yet more colour from the great, grey buildings.

A small paper boat bobbed along in the stream of rainwater, spinning in the occasional eddy of the gutter before flipping onto its side and disappearing down a drain. It bobbed for a few seconds in the dark tunnel then set off again, turning left then right through the maze beneath London's streets until at last it came to rest against a small iron grate.

The upper point of its folded paper sail brushed a small brass bell that tinkled softly. After a few moments the grate opened and a hand reached out to lift it inside.

The boat was carried through dry cellars, lined with books as old as England, and up flagstone steps, bowed through centuries of footfall. Finally it was placed on a small wooden desk where more hands unfolded it and ran it under a hot iron – where it steamed gently – before it was rolled up, placed in a wooden cylinder and corked.

The cylinder was pushed into a brass tube and away it sped. The tubes ran throughout the building. No room was left uncovered, and all cylinders knew exactly where they were going.

This particular cylinder was headed for a room where a lady sat at a large mahogany desk. Her back was so straight it was difficult to tell where her chair ended and her spine began. Her dress was heavily starched. The creases in every fold appeared so sharp they could cut you, and the white bun of her hair was so perfectly shaped that you could be mistaken for thinking that she was expertly balancing a ball on the back of her head.

At the thunk of the message tube, the lady looked up over her half-spectacles, reached out a kidney-spotted hand and uncorked it with such grace it looked like juggling, except not as vulgar.

She carefully unrolled and read the note contained within, sat back in her chair and considered a large map of the world, displayed along one wall of the otherwise sparse room.

The map was suitably coloured with the political leanings of each country. She noted with satisfaction that most of it was still pink and therefore a part of the British Empire. The surface was covered with a series of finely-crafted push-pin flags, and even from this great distance she seemed to be studying them, until her eyes eventually fell on one and she smiled.

'Harry,' she said to herself, with great warmth in her voice.

Content with her find, she placed her hands neatly in her lap and coughed. At once the door opened and a younger version of herself came into the room. The new arrival was identical in every way, apart from her face being somewhat less lined and her hair being slightly less snow-white and more silver-grey.

The new woman did not leave the doorway. Behind her, a warmer-coloured corridor led away, lined with large red wooden doors, all marked with brass Roman numerals. There was a young lady sat on a bench just along the corridor, who looked past the woman in the doorway and gave the older matriarch a small smile. The old woman, almost unnoticeably, sniffed with momentary derision at this breach of protocol.

'Yes Mother?' said the woman in the doorway, a pad and pencil held tightly in her hands.

'Get me the vain one,' the old lady instructed, with little emotion in her aged, cracked voice.

'I'm afraid she's on a mission with some banker's children, Mother,' said the standing lady.

'The animal wrangler?'

'Sorting out a widower.'

'The wayward nun?'

There was a moment's pause. 'Just taken holy orders.'

'Hettie?' The older woman's voice seemed a little fraught, but only to the trained ear.

'Staking out the Natural History Museum, Mother.'

'I'm sure she has her reasons. Do we have *any* agents free?'

'We have the new girl.'

With this, the young lady in the corridor leant out once more, peering past the secretary, and gave a small wave.

The one known as 'Mother' looked into space for a long time and then to the map once more. She gave an audible sigh.

'Send her in.'

The desk filled most of the room, and the chair before it was certainly shorter than the average but not so much as to cause offence. The walls of the office were panelled to about half their height and were then sensibly striped with wallpaper. On one wall was a sculpted Omega symbol surmounted by a closed umbrella with the letters NANI beneath it.

There was only one window and this was behind the desk, overlooking an inner courtyard and throwing the older lady into almost perfect silhouette. There were no clocks, but there was a handstand and an elephant foot with a single umbrella standing in it.

The girl chose not to sit, because she had not been asked, and she also knew the power of a shorter chair.

'What is your name, child?'

The girl who stood before Mother was about average height, with light auburn hair cut into a stylish bob. She wore a maroon coat that covered a dark purple, sensibly-tailored dress and a purple hat, with a brim slightly too wide for Mother's liking. The umbrella in her hand matched her outfit's colours, with bold wide stripes, and the handle was topped with the sculpted head of a stargazing hare. Her shoes were black and highly polished and so far were the only thing that met with Mother's approval.

'Beatrix Honey, ma'am,' said the girl in a friendly manner.

'Do I look like the Queen? No I do not. You shall address me as Mother.'

'Oh, I assumed you were actually the other lady's mother.'

'Really? Do you make assumptions often?'

There was a pause as the girl thought for a moment.

'I believe I do. Yes.'

Mother seemed surprised with the answer and looked the girl straight in the eyes.

'Was I right? I often am,' Miss Honey said, without breaking eye contact, and for the first time, Mother was visibly shaken.

'You will be sent out from here to join a group of nannies and governesses looking after a small Russian family. They do not know you are coming but will need to accept you as being an honest and legitimate employee. You will be provided with all the latest equipment and will report back anything you feel is of importance, and also everything you do not believe is important in the slightest.

'You will protect the children with your life. I will pass on the mission brief to your superior and she will make sure you are completely aware of the seriousness of this situation. Do I make myself clear, Nanny Honey?'

The girl smiled and nodded. She instinctively felt this was the moment to take her leave, and she always trusted her instincts, so she headed for the door. Just as she reached the handle, Mother spoke again,

'You assumed correctly, and that is a gift. Use it well.'

5
CHANGES

Iron couldn't believe it. He was on a Zeppelin heading toward Berlin and everyone was treating him like nobility.

Two days before, he had been a simple foundling, working the estate of his benefactor Lord Branding, pretending that he was actually the Lord of the manor from a long line of knighted heroes, just waiting for his chance to uphold the family honour. And now it had almost happened!

The Lord was certainly a kindly man; though most of the good deeds he did were conceived from the opinion they would improve his standing in society.

The Branding Institute for City Foundlings had been where Iron had grown up. Lord Branding had opened the Institute to impress Lady Em, but he had swiftly realised that he had no idea of what to do with foundlings once they had been found.

He had chosen to have these boys and girls educated privately in the classical style to begin with, but as they were commoners, he realised it would do them no good in later life. So the moment they could work, Lord Branding had set his new charges to learn some useful task, to assist with the running of the estate.

Iron had been drafted into making sure anything mechanical that needed to run did so correctly, and if it needed to be driven, then he would do that too.

A steward offered Iron a canapé as he looked out of the window at the rolling clouds, wishing he could actually touch them. Unfortunately the poor steward had started by calling Iron 'Sir' to get his attention. When there was no response, the steward tried 'Lord Branding', as that was the name under which Iron was now travelling.

Iron looked around, expecting to see the portly Lord stood there, having changed his mind on the chance of adventure, only to realise that the steward meant him.

He apologetically took the canapé and looked at it with disdain. It had the appearance of a tiny unfinished fish pie, not even enough to fill a kitten's stomach, and he had the hunger of a lion on him.

Iron was going to have to get used to all of this, especially the name. He'd been called Iron for 15 years, and that was the only name he had ever known. He could only assume that Lord Branding had tired of names, as he had so many of his own, and had therefore taken to naming his foundlings after the various industries he owned.

Iron had technically grown up with three brothers; Coal, Barley and Butcher. Luckily for his sister, Lord Branding had recently traded his Whitstable oyster factory for a cotton plantation. It had been a shame to say farewell to his fellow foundlings, but Cotton had kissed him fondly on the cheek and waved until he was out of sight. So, Iron knew he wouldn't be forgotten.

Besides, he could most certainly get used to this lifestyle, even though the hastily-altered tweed suit itched quite badly and the canapé tasted mainly of salt.

Iron unfolded the documents from the Royal Order of Dragons and read through them once again.

Lord Branding,

It is a great honour for you to protect the Empire on behalf of the Royal Order of Dragons, but it must be impressed upon you that we are a secret society and all accolades will be awarded to you only by your peers and never by the wider public. Any attempt to impart to others your mission or the missions of the Order will result in your immediate disappearance. Therefore all further communication will be performed in a clandestine manner.

Your first task will be to travel to Berlin and to book in at the Hotel Dansk, where your further mission, and any equipment needed, will be waiting for you.

We salute you and your work sir.

Protego.

Iron's education had extended to Latin, and he was aware the last word was not a signature but instead the motto of the Dragons. It meant simply: 'To

Protect'.

He smiled at the thought as they descended through the clouds; and as he saw the streets of Berlin laid out below them, his excitement grew.

The vast metal crab moved through the water. Rudolph Diesel had decided almost immediately on hearing the news, that staying in one location was a bad idea.

Diesel shook his head as he read the tickertape message again. How could the possible peacemaker be dead? The details were sketchy, but that made it even worse, as already blame was starting to fly.

He had panicked and sent out gifts to the heads of the bruised states, hoping to heal any slight they thought had been done against them, but it was flippant to think that presents could distract nervous and uncertain nations from possible war.

Luckily only one of the gifts had been sent when the Head of Security and pointed out that any gift from DB1 would actually arm the recipient with the latest technology ... He would make sure that their agents in Germany intercepted the 'gift' so it wouldn't reach the German government. It would then be taken away and destroyed.

The thing to do now was to accept that simply monitoring radio signals wasn't working, and to start to create some stealthy machines that they could send out to patrol the world looking for signs.

Diesel summoned his fellow scientists. It was time for a briefing.

Iron was looking for signs too. His German wasn't as

polished as he'd hoped, and his inbuilt desire to not waste money on a cab had resulted in him becoming hopelessly lost in the streets of Berlin. He had dragged his travel trunk for many miles, and he was dishevelled and hot before finally finding his hotel in the late evening. This was only after a friendly grocer, with a passing knowledge of English, had practically walked him there.

The Hotel Dansk was tall, imposing and most certainly not the sort of establishment that would have let Iron through its doors a week earlier. Now, a man in fine livery with hair so slicked down it looked painted on was holding the door while another rushed to take his trunk.

He felt himself getting taller as he walked to reception. The desk clerk most certainly had the look of a man up a lot later than he thought check-in should be finished by, but he was putting a professional face on it.

The language barrier led to some misunderstandings, but Iron finally got checked in, and then discovered that there was a message for him. The clerk, with a large smile, grateful that the ordeal of translating fractured German was finally over, handed Iron a brown manila envelope, seemingly fat with papers.

Iron turned it over in his hands, a puzzled expression on his face. The clerk looked quizzical and broke his normal rule of speaking only German to the guests.

'Iz zis not vot you vunted, sir?'

Iron tried not to look disappointed. 'I was hoping for … a box,' he said, happy to get his tongue straight again, despite the lack of secret Order equipment.

'A box, sir? How big iz zis box?'

The young lad looked a bit embarrassed. 'I've no idea, just a box … possibly heavy.'

The clerk raised a single finger and walked with purpose to the doorman. A short conversation saw both men leave the hotel briefly, and when the clerk reappeared, his smile returned.

'Ve haf a box, sir. It appears to 'ave somehow been left in ze side passage. My doorman iz attending to eet and vill have eet fetched to your room.'

Iron grinned and thanked the clerk profusely before almost skipping to his room, happy as a boy on Christmas morning.

He jiggled the key in the lock and pushed open the door. What he saw stopped him dead in his tracks. The room was the most stunning space he had ever seen. Lord Branding's home of course was a beautiful place full of antiques and paintings displayed in large airy rooms with ceilings so high you couldn't touch them even if you leapt, but it was still tatty around the edges, with the smell and colour attributed to frequent cigar smoke and what Lord Branding called 'ancestry'.

Here, moulded details were picked out in gold leaf and the walls were hand-painted with delicate patterns. The furniture was new but had the quality of tomorrow's antiques. Furthermore, one wall was a bank of finally-crafted windows, and beyond was the impressive, panoramic vista of the Berlin skyline.

Iron stood there looking at the room and the view, and he would probably have stood there for hours if the doorman, complete with large wooden box, hadn't arrived behind him.

In the luxurious room the box looked out of place. Its sides were clean and neatly cut but it was still a packing crate, no matter how you looked at it. The only thing that gave it an identity was a burnt-on logo: the stylised head of a Greek goddess, possibly Athena, although, thought Iron, it could just have easily have been Britannia.

Iron wondered why the Dragons didn't use a dragon symbol but then guessed it would too easily give the game away.

Before he opened the box, Iron drew the curtains, reluctantly shutting out the magnificent view.

The box was as tall as a man and resembled a wardrobe in many ways, making it easy to prise open, once you'd worked out which side the hinges were on.

Inside, it was packed with straw matting, which Iron took in both hands and eagerly pulled free. Then, for the second time that night, Iron paused, not quite able to believe his eyes.

The box appeared to contain a manikin, and when the likeness of a body is revealed in any coffin-like shape, it is sure to stop even the most furious paper-ripper in his pursuit of presents.

The reality was a helmet and sculpted body parts held together by cables and pistons. To Iron's eyes it looked just like the suit of armour he had craved throughout his childhood.

Reaching in, he lifted up the helmet like a precious crown and brought it out into the light of the room. It was easy to see that it had been sculpted to cover the entire head, but to add little in the way of bulk. The visor was designed in the style of Samurai helmets, it had a sculpted face-plate complete with a real hair moustache, but the modern twist was the eye slits, which were covered with aviation-style goggles.

He slipped it over his head and was surprised at how light and comfortable it felt, despite clearly being made of iron. It was even riveted together in places.

Leaving it on, he slowly removed the other items from the crate and slipped them on over his clothes. Finally, turning to the mirror, Iron smiled at the sight that greeted him. The body parts fitted snugly over his chest, shoulders, knees and elbows and included medieval style gauntlets as well as boot stirrups.

Every part was joined to its neighbour with hydraulic pistons that moved and enhanced Iron's natural movements, producing a satisfying hiss and saving him a lot of energy.

He made the mistake of doing a little jump, and leapt so high that he hit the ceiling with a crash. The next few minutes were spent standing there, nervously waiting for a knock on his door and his instant expulsion from this amazing room, but none came.

Iron turned back to the box and the three strange items that remained within it. The first was a chunky backpack, constructed of two bulky cylinders tapered to points. Iron studied this carefully. It was either a boiler for heat or had some other use, perhaps linked to the two other objects.

The second was a box, clearly a control panel of some sort, which had clips that hooked it onto the chest of the suit and cables that could be connected to the helmet and to the backpack.

The final object was obviously a weapon. It was held in the hand and went over the forearm and featured barrels that made it look a little like a Gatling gun. There was a rear chamber that rattled and, on inspection, Iron found to be full of ball bearings. The trigger was a grip worn on the palm, which kept the wearer's fingers well away from the barrels. The weapon also plugged by cable into the control panel; and, once he had it all connected and set up, Iron felt somewhat invincible. This beat any partridge hunting rifle hands down.

With the security of someone who knows they are not being watched, Iron acted out a series of scenarios before his floor-length mirror. He tracked an imaginary enemy across the room. Jumped and leaped around with the agility of a monkey, and crouched, ducked and dived to avoid incoming fire. It was only when sunlight started to show through the curtains that he reluctantly removed the suit and made his way to the room's four poster bed, which had started to look like the most comfortable space in the world.

As his eyes started to close, he realised that he hadn't yet read his mission documents but vowed he'd do it the moment he woke up.

Iron was asleep almost as soon as his head hit the pillow. He slept soundly and dreamed happily of dragons and princesses, and of men in fantastic armour who came bounding to the rescue.

6
MONKEY BUSINESS

Flyn poured a large gin into a crystal glass and set it on a small table, before arranging a selection of biscuits and cakes on an elegant stand and placing it beside the drink. The flybrid pushed the biscuits about for a while with a white gloved hand, before quickly grabbing several and pushing them noisily into his mouth.

The action didn't go unnoticed and Flyn was suddenly clipped around the back of his fly-like head by a delicate hand that felt like stone. The mutant butler took this as his cue to leave and shuffled from the room with his head hung low.

Igor went back to studying the maps with the doctor, her tresses phasing from jet black to a softer chestnut. The whole table was laid out with small models representing the possible armies of the world, ranging in shades of grey, from the pure white figures set up for Tripp's steam allies to black for countries caught up fully in the grip of diesel.

'If we can just find a tipping point, we can make them all fight each other; it will certainly save on our involvement,' the doctor said, moving a large white monster figure across the map. 'Really, whoever would have thought a rampaging sheep could get everyone so hot under the collar?'

Igor watched the doctor's enthusiasm grow as he played with the figures.

The doctor had always been good to her, ever since she had been found as a child, washed up on an English beach, and she had vowed always to be there for him.

He had mood swings, that was true. Most often he would be full of light as he created his inventions, serums and cocktails. It was in one of these moods that he had designed her tank and given her the freedom to follow him around. But then there were the other times, when he could be dark and melancholic, as he considered the destruction of his beloved British Empire, a world of craftsmanship and steam.

She glided toward the map, picking up two of the doctor's monster figures, before placing them down: one on Germany and the other on Russia.

Tripps looked over and smiled. 'Igor, you clever little fish, that's genius.'

Igor smiled. 'I'll get the cocktails,' she said, and glided out of the study.

Tripps regarded the figures on the map and started to consider which might be the perfect creatures for the job. The sheep had been a simple monster, its brain difficult to control, but these behemoths would have to make an impact. Not just on those they squashed into the ground but on everyone that saw them lumber past. Russia would have to believe beyond a shadow of a doubt that they were dealing with a creature from Germany, and *vice versa*.

By the time Igor returned with the mobile lab,

clinking with test tubes and alive with colourful liquids, Dr Tripps was already surrounded by books, laughing to himself as he turned the pages, taking notes.

The blackboard was soon wheeled over, and Tripps sketched furiously as ideas took shape. The clouds outside the large, round window scudded past, and the sky turned from beautiful blue, through a rainbow of reds as the sun set, before finally becoming dark as moonlight flooded into the room.

As the sun rose once again on the ingenious doctor and his beautiful assistant, the blackboard now bore two striking pictures, rendered in great detail, and labelled 'Berlin Bear' and 'Moscow Mule'.

One table was full of scientific apparatus: glass beakers, vials and tubes full of gently steaming and bubbling liquids. At the end of the apparatus, liquids dripped into two similarly-labelled bottles. Berlin Bear was a rich blue, while Moscow Mule was a gingery amber. With the cocktail brewing nicely, Tripps and Igor walked out onto the deck to watch the sunrise.

Even after all these years, very few changes had been made to the *Arc*. It still had a large, gas-filled balloon high above it, although this was now so patched that it looked as if it had never been of one type of fabric. The *Arc* itself had been painted many times; a protection against weather rather than a vanity of appearance.

The only real addition was a giant gun mounted on the fore-deck. It had the look of any gun emplacement found on a battleship, although there was a seat with levers for the operator and a selection of barrels. The ornate brass barrel that was on top held a large whaling harpoon, which was in turn tethered by an aged but strong rope.

It hadn't taken the crew of the *Arc* long to discover that they were not alone in the heavens, and they protected themselves often against hungry air kraken and curious sky whales. They had also noted that more human folk were exploring the skies, and on more than one occasion the doctor had defended his air space rights like some sort of pirate. Far below, the land mass of Europe unfolded, its people unaware of the danger to them all, high above in the skies, hidden behind the clouds of its own making.

As the doctor and Igor watched the Sun lighten the day, they were passed by a group of small monkeys. All had impressive wings on their backs and carried an assortment of nets and spears. The leader, who was slightly larger than the others, saluted the doctor, who saluted back; and, as a squadron, they launched into the air in search of food for the larder.

Tripps linked arms with Igor.

'When we have returned the world to steam, my ocean princess, I should like to retire here and build a home in the clouds.' He pointed back in the direction of Hawaii. 'The air is warm above the volcanic islands and our cloud city nears completion. We could even grow children.'

In the distance, a small timer pinged. 'Ah! The cocktails are complete. Let's go and destroy something.'

The doctor worked quickly, decanting the liquids into appropriate bottles and storing the rest for future use. He called out for a LUMP, and then remembered that they had all headed off to hunt.

'Blast it. Igor, could you fetch me the monkey-o-matic, please.'

Igor nodded obediently, putting down the book

she was reading. She glided across to a cabinet, took out a small apparatus that looked a little like a clock and placed it onto Tripps' desk. Alongside it, the doctor placed something covered in a black cloth. With a flourish like a stage magician's assistant revealing his trick, Igor lifted the cover, uncovering a bell jar containing two miniature Tesla coils.

Tripps removed a small key on a chain from around his neck, unlocked a drawer in a writing bureau against the wall and removed a small wooden box full of tiny bottles.

The device Igor had placed on the desk was mainly wooden in construction and featured on the front a dial that was clearly and neatly marked up with a selection of choices. There was a rust mark where the small metal arrow had left a stain on the glass, indicating that it had been set to 'flying' for a very long time.

Tripps moved a lever on the side to '2' and then considered the bottles he was holding. 'They could be a bit heavy. Let's go all the way up to three on size, I think.'

He moved the lever to its final position, marked with a '3'. Taking a small bottle of green glowing liquid marked 'Shem', he pierced the cork with a hollow needle before placing it in one of the brass pipes on the side of the machine.

Then he lifted up a bottle from the box marked 'Rhesus', but found it was quite empty apart from a slight red stain to the glass.

'Oh bother,' the doctor said, peering at the empty vial, 'are we out of Rhesus again? Remind me we need to go on a jungle trip, Igor, or we're only one big storm away from being crewless!'

He ran his fingers over the other bottles, and

pulled out one by fate alone. It was marked 'Howler'.

'Oh goodness me, no.' He put it back with a shudder. He had never been an admirer of the folks who raised their voices, as they generally had nothing of worth to say. He had avoided that element of society for many years and wasn't going to remind himself of them by creating their primate equivalent.

'Third time's a charm,' he muttered, selecting another bottle. The full scarlet vial that was lifted from the box was clearly marked 'Baboon'.

'Perfect,' crooned the doctor as he prepared his needle and pierced the cork.

The liquid was again placed in one of the brass pipes.

Cranking a small brass handle on the side of the machine, the smiling Tripps then flipped up four levers beneath the dial, connecting them into a brass plate, where they touched with a little spark.

After a short pause, the Tesla coils started to hum. A crack of lightning fizzed within the bell jar, and what looked like a hairy egg covered in mucus appeared.

Bubbles worked their way to the top of both bottles. Igor quickly removed the egg and replaced the dome. Another lightning crack, one more egg and two more bubbles. Tripps disengaged the levers and looked at Igor. He seemed very pleased with the result.

'And it's now safely off,' he said, noting that Igor's hair went briefly pink as if she were blushing.

Tripps took the two eggs and carefully placed them on the floor. They were growing larger even as he held them.

On the floor, both eggs moved, not cracking but unfolding and growing the entire time. One appeared for a while just to be getting larger, until it finally yawned, displaying a huge set of teeth and canine fangs. The other egg was becoming more a big ball of fur with large vulture-like wings and a huge purple bottom. A twisted, lithe arm shot from the yawning egg, followed by another as it stretched, and two yellow eyes popped open just above the mouth.

After a few more pops, cracks and odd gurgling noises, a large pair of winged baboons sat in the middle of the study floor, looking about them like eager dogs. As quick as a flash, Igor slipped two small control crowns onto their heads and they both stood bolt upright, eyes straight ahead.

Trips looked intensely at the two apes, his cranium tank glowing and bubbling, his face set in concentration, and their eyes glazed over.

Tripps addressed the apes: 'You are no longer Largely Universal Monkey Personnel. LUMP One, you will now think of yourself as "Gruber" and will be an embodiment of the German people.'

The baboon saluted sharply, snapping its heels together.

'LUMP Two,' continued Tripps, turning his attention to the second ape, 'you shall be known as "Peter" and encompass the feelings of the Russian people.'

The other ape punched a fist into the sky and gave the now-German fellow a shifty sideways look.

'You will now fly to your respective countries and try to find a resident that matches your ideals and force them to drink the liquid I now give you. However, if you feel your mission will be compromised or you find no-one with the right outlook, you will take the cocktail yourself. Is your mission clear to you?'

Both baboons nodded.

'Then fly, my collaborators, fly!'

The baboons jostled toward the window, taking the bottles from Tripps as they went, and launched themselves into the air. They flew twice around the *Arc* to get their bearings, then separated off into the clouds.

Tripps smiled. 'Right Igor, let's go to the war room and get me hooked up. I have a game to play.'

7
RUSSIAN ROULETTE

Beatrix had enjoyed her journey from England immensely and was now travelling in an open-topped car from the station to Alexander Palace, the current home of the Romanovs. She felt very regal. She would be joining the already well-interned British nanny, Miss Coster, who had been an agent for the National Army of Nursery Intelligence for many years.

Beatrix alighted from the car, smiling up at the façade of the grand palace. She was met at the door by Miss Coster, a friendly woman with a bosom that would have brought tears to most men's eyes and pain to most women's backs. The only things that were larger were her smile and her friendly handshake, and she seemed to know how to use them all. The smile and bosom definitely helped in persuading the chauffer to carry all of Beatrix's bags up four flights of stairs to her room.

'Well it's certainly refreshing to have some new blood around here,' said Miss Coster. 'Nanny King is often intoxicated in the evening and I could do with some talk of home. I think it will be best if you just call me Nana around here as it will save the children becoming confused, although they all know Nanny King as just that.'

She paused for a second, presumably to catch breath, and flashed her award-winning smile at the man struggling with the bags into the small room that was to be Beatrix's refuge. The room was equipped with a writing desk, chair, bed and wardrobe. It had a tiny window that opened up to reveal rooftops stretching away into the distance.

'It's not much, I know, but I shall help you move in, and tomorrow I will introduce you to the children. You can help me with their English by telling them of home. It will be a nice change for me, and they are still like sponges at this stage, the little poppets.'

Miss Coster, whom Beatrix forced herself to think of as Nana, ushered the chauffer from the room before he too could get comfortable. The moment the door closed, Nana embraced Beatrix. 'Oh my! A fellow agent. It has been such a long time, and a struggle too. Everybody in this country seems to have it in for my little charges. I've despatched several would-be assassins already, and this country has any number of bogeymen lurking under the bed. No-one knew you were coming, so I have not one jot of information about you, or why you're here. I had to let the chauffer there believe you were simply new staff, but I'm guessing there is a big threat coming.'

Beatrix was almost stunned by the assault of words from the fellow agent, so held up her hand to get a moment of quiet before she spoke. Nana sat down on the bed and allowed the girl to compose herself.

'My name is Beatrix Honey, my friends call me Bea and my charges call me Nanny Honey.' She took a breath to prove to herself that conversations didn't need to be rushed, even in situations like this. 'I have been sent here by Mother because there is a firm belief that a plot to throw the world into war has been launched. The children, as always, are considered a target.'

She stopped again, went to the door and, after a moment, opened it suddenly. Happy that they were indeed alone, she closed the door and continued: 'Monsters are being used.'

Nana let out an audible gasp. 'Being used openly?'

'Oh yes,' said Beatrix, barely raising her eyebrows, hoping it gave her a look of a seasoned agent. 'Monster activity has been noted to have increased in several locations around the globe, and many have been suffering from a form of gigantism.'

With this news Nana stood suddenly, her bosom bouncing, and went to the window.

'Will they come here, do you think?'

'Oh, most certainly. That's why I've been sent. I'm fully equipped.' Beatrix tapped the travel bag with her umbrella. 'It's now just a case of playing the waiting game ...'

The next morning, Beatrix awoke bright and early. She washed in the shared bathroom with Nana, who spoke constantly about building traps. It seemed that Nana was quite the inventor and had used her skills to make the bathtubs a lot more comfortable for the children, and herself, with the introduction of a removable flannel seat that kept sensitive bottoms off the cold marble.

She was more than happy to turn those same skills to building traps and defences against monsters, although she let it be known in no uncertain terms that she thought that if there was any monster around, it would most certainly be the Tsarina's mystic, a man named Grigori Rasputin.

'What do you mean the Tsarina's mystic?' enquired Bea, once she and Nana were alone again. Magic was always openly discussed with the agents of NANI, but she had heard no talk of magic at the Romanovs' palace.

'Well, when the Tsarevich Alexi became ill, his mother would trust anyone who offered a cure; that's certainly how that monster Rasputin got invited in here. He says he's a monk, but no monk I have ever met acts like him.'

Bea was intrigued. 'I know we shall be busy with lessons this morning, but maybe I should go and have a look at this Rasputin in the afternoon.'

Nana agreed that this was a very good idea.

The English lesson had been wonderful. The children were so well behaved and hung on Nanny Honey's every word. They clearly loved Nana, who remained strict but friendly. She playfully told them she would hand them to the Japanese whenever they showed signs of misbehaviour, and the children would dutifully sit straight-backed and polite at the very thought.

Just before they stopped for lunch, the room grew noticeably colder. Looking up, Bea saw a figure standing in the doorway. He was tall and wore long robes of fine material, but his hair was straggly and unkempt, and his long black beard cast his face into darkness. All his features were in shadow except his eyes, which caught the light and stared unblinking at Nanny Honey.

Beatrix felt uncomfortable before the gaze, but

called on all her British reserve not to show any sign of unease. Suddenly, without saying a word, the man turned and was gone. The children instantly started whispering amongst themselves. Nana gave Bea a long, knowing look, before she turned toward the classroom and mentioned the Japanese again.

The encounter had been most unsettling.

That afternoon, Nanny Honey wasn't needed, because Nanny King finally showed her face – which was fronted by a nose that glowed red as though sunburnt – and took over the lessons. With some free time and now regarded as a member of staff, Beatrix felt that she could wander the grounds and do some discreet investigation of her own.

It wasn't long before she located the scary monk. He was acting as if he was the head of the household, ordering the staff about as he prepared for a trip. On enquiring, Beatrix was shocked to discover he was planning on visiting his wife and children. She was suddenly very aware of why Nana had considered him not a typical monk. All monks she knew were sworn to a vow of chastity in their service to God.

She raced to her room and gathered her belongings, leaving a note for Nana on her whereabouts. Then she headed into the stable yard, where she knew they were preparing Rasputin's carriage, and asked a stable boy if there was any way she could travel into town. The boy started to dust off a bike for her, but she had asked clearly and knowingly in the monk's hearing. He didn't react at first, but as the bike was given a final polish, he turned.

'You will strap your bicycle to my carriage and I

will drop you in town,' he said in heavily accented Russian, more as a command than as a friendly offer.

'That's all right, I haven't seen the countryside yet, I'm happy to ride.'

At Bea's comment, the whole stable fell quiet, including the horses, and everyone looked at Rasputin.

He stared at her. 'My offer was not a request,' he said. 'Unless of course you were riding into town in search of a new job?'

Bea was happy that her ploy had paid off. She hadn't wanted Rasputin to think the ride was what she had desired all along, as he might be less relaxed. She shrugged and let the stable boy take the freshly-cleaned bike and tie it onto the back of the royal carriage before she clambered inside.

After a while, Rasputin also entered the carriage and sat opposite her. He sat in the middle of the seat and filled the whole carriage with his dark presence. He didn't say a word, but once again his eyes were on Bea, hypnotic with an inner light of their own. She felt the desire to button her coat fully up to the neck and hold it tightly about her, but she resisted and looked out of the window instead.

They pulled away and travelled for a couple of miles without anyone speaking. The driveway from the house was smooth, but soon they passed between the magnificent gateposts and the sentry boxes of the Tsar's personal guard, and the road turned to the bumpier concourse of the countryside. The thin trees were numerous and came right up to the road's edge, branches joined above them like a tunnel, and occasionally brushed the top of the carriage as it passed.

It was Rasputin who broke the silence.

'You are very young to be a nanny,' he said,

steepling his fingers before his mouth as if praying.

'I'm 16, sir. More than old enough to look after children.' Beatrix looked briefly at the monk, before again returning her gaze to the passing countryside, suddenly uncomfortable. 'I have been looking after children for a few years now. I don't believe my age has ever been an issue.'

She said this almost as an aside, not directing it at the monk, and tried to keep the hurt out of her voice, which was somewhat easier in stilted Russian.

'However …' she turned back to Rasputin, 'you don't exactly fall nicely into the box marked "monk".'

Rasputin was quiet for a moment and then burst out into the most tremendous laughter that filled the carriage and chased away the darkness, surprisingly casting the man in a very different light from the brooding presence he portrayed at court.

The laughter stopped with uncanny sharpness when the carriage suddenly pulled up short and bumped and jostled the occupants against the sides. Outside, the horses whinnied and snorted, the driver cursed.

Rasputin was out of the door with lightning quickness and Beatrix was right behind him, suddenly not wanting to let the monk out of her sight. She didn't want to know what he was capable of doing to someone who displeased him, and feared for the driver.

Rasputin shouted up at the man behind the horses. 'What is wrong with you, are you an imbecile?'

The driver was looking off the road. 'There was a creature, sir. It shot across the road like a giant bird into the trees, and spooked the horses. I feared we would hit it, but I think it got away without injury.'

'And you chose to not just run it down? There is

enough wildlife in this country that we can afford to spare some and not interrupt my journey.'

'It wasn't natural though, sir. It was like a big, shaggy dog with wings. I was frightened it would hurt the horses or damage the carriage.'

Rasputin laughed again. 'A shaggy dog story, as the British would say.' He turned to Beatrix, who was standing at the forest edge. 'You seem keen to see our monster. Shall we go look together and get a story for the children?'

Beatrix was aware of the dangers of entering a strange wood with a man of Rasputin's reputation and sudden mood swings. She suddenly felt a long way from home. But she had known the dark streets of London for many years, and what would have scared a foreigner there didn't bother her one jot. So, to regain an element of control, she raised her umbrella, motioned to the wood and chirruped in her chirpiest cockney accent: 'Walk on Guv'nor.' She then disappeared into the trees, followed by the smiling monk, who, to the coach driver, suddenly looked a lot more threatening and sinister than the creature he had just swerved to avoid.

8

MONSTER MASH

Despite the clear instructions given them by Tripps, both baboons had headed straight for Russia. Gruber wanted a quick attack against his assigned target and thought it best to be close, while Peter was headed to find the perfect Russian subject for the cocktail.

On the hills surrounding Moscow, the baboon now known as Gruber landed. His mind was fixed and strangely efficient. A level of order had entered every one of his actions, unfolding them into precise plans. He would not find someone appropriate to give his cocktail to, so he uncorked the bottle and downed the entire contents himself with a noisy gulping.

Gruber already knew he was a fighter as he struggled against the fatigue that washed over him, but now he was a thinker too, and he was hoping to experience every change in his body. The reality was that Tripps had included a sleeping draught in each cocktail. Rigorous testing had taught the doctor that the change would unhinge any mind and stop his ability to control the questing beast, thus sleep was the best way to allow the change to happen without destroying the mind of the subject.

High above Europe's contoured scenery, Tripps was making himself comfortable in his leather chair. He was linked back into the brain-enhancing machine with its tubes and cables, and he focused his mind to see what was happening in the world. He received a brief glimpse of the sheep monster's mind, erratic and underdeveloped, before he felt something new growing. There were no senses yet, just the feel of a vast frame stretching out. Cells replicating, mutating and becoming the creature the doctor had conceived on his blackboard only the night before. He could feel his excitement increasing as the bear-like creature slowly became aware. It had some differences from his initial design as the fresh baboon DNA struggled to make its mark on the cocktail's ursine building blocks.

Gruber's mind was so hidden down inside the psyche of the beast that Tripps gained control with ease.

Struggling at first to stand, the giant bearboon creature rose unsteadily up on its dark-furred, tree-like hind legs before gaining full control of its posture and rearing up to its full height. Its fur was so black and fresh upon its body that a blue sheen ran across it as it moved in the sunlight. Its forearms were longer than hoped for, so movement seemed easier in a semi-quadrupedal walk, much like that of a mountain gorilla. Its back legs were short and bowed, and as much as Tripps tried to make it go straight forward, any burst of speed would make it turn almost sideways. The face featured a pleasingly long muzzle and its teeth had become so fang-like and large that the mouth couldn't close without resembling some medieval portcullis slamming shut.

Tripps could feel the huge humped arch of the creature's back. Approaching Moscow, the slope he walked down overbalanced the strangely-shaped monster and it toppled forward, rolling down the hill like a circus acrobat, before arriving at the bottom, crushing what turned out to be greenhouses beneath its gargantuan frame.

Moscow was wrapped up in its own unfolding day of fish markets, so the great crash on the outskirts of town and the resultant rising dust cloud went unnoticed. Dr Tripps instructed the beast to roar, and all 30 foot of the bearboon bunched up, before letting out a tremendous bellow.

It must have been excessively loud, because Igor clearly heard its faint echo from where she stood in the *Arc* above Europe. The people of Moscow raised their weary heads and gazed out of town, toward whatever trouble seemed to be heading their way. At the same time, every bird in Moscow took flight and swirled overhead in a vast black cloud before heading off in the opposite direction.

What appeared above the sculpted domes along the river was the twisted evil of the bearboon. It was at once familiar to the assembled people, and yet at the same time completely alien.

For years, political illustrators had given the warlike nations of the world personalities. The greater a nation became, the more monstrous the caricature. As the Berlin bearboon sent a huge fist crashing through the roof of an outlying temple, not one Russian standing watching in aghast horror was in any doubt about the beast's origin.

Tripps was laughing manically in his chair. His hands twitched like the legs of a dreaming dog as he started his reign of destruction. The temples were almost too good to ignore, with their metal domes of varied colour and design. He pulled at one and it broke cleanly away from the tower it surmounted.

Tripps was taken by how much the dome looked like the *piklehaube* helmets favoured by the German military's high command, with its large eagle design and pointed apex, and in a moment of manic genius slipped it up and onto the bearboon's head.

The trap was complete. As far as every red-blooded Muscovite was aware, they were under attack from Germany. Every superstitious Cossack knew that the forests of Germany were full of monsters and giants. It was the most despicable enemy that would train one of these aberrations against God and send it to Moscow to destroy their places of worship.

They knew that this creature must have been responsible for the train wreck, which now had their allies publicly apologising for something that wasn't their fault. It was a conspiracy to create war, and they believed Germany was throwing the first punch.

The great beast tore through the castle-like buildings by the river. Moscow had clearly been built to last, and as much as it tried to smash down years of history, it was mainly cosmetic damage that the bearboon did to the ancient structures.

Frustrated, and not wishing to be defeated, Tripps focused on the people that ran from his creation like ants fleeing a disturbed nest. It was a simple action to pick up one of the beast's misshapen feet and bring it stamping down on the crowd below.

Things squished between its toes and Tripps got the feeling that this was what it must be like to step on jelly. This jelly contained small, sharp sticks however, that made the beast roar in discomfort. The sudden shooting pain in his foot made Tripps relax his mental hold, and Gruber sprang forward to wrest control. He had been more than happy to ride along as a passenger and watch the carnage unfold, but Tripps most certainly couldn't feel the pain – he had thoughtfully installed dampers against that in his mental control – and it was this that gave Gruber the edge.

The bearboon turned and sat down on the city wall, pulling his foot up in its big ape-like hands to inspect the damage. Brushing away the gore and detritus, that had possibly once been morning worshippers, Gruber could now clearly see the splinter-like bones that stuck from the sole of his giant foot. He used his fingers to scratch an edge and pull the offending items out, casting the bone fragments aside to land gruesomely amongst the fleeing, and now hysterically screaming, residents.

By the time he was happy and vowing not to step on any more people, without at least a rethink on caution or big shoes, the city had cleared. All except for the Russian soldiers, who had filed into a suitable courtyard to set up their lines of defence with quiet military precision and were even now setting up three highly-disciplined lines of volley from troops armed with the latest muskets.

Count Ilya Rostov had command. He raised his arm and gave the order to fire. The blast from the front line created a sudden cloud of smoke and flame. The Berlin bear was peppered with shot and it hurt. Gruber bent down and threw his arms wide, letting out a roar of such power that some of the soldiers lost their helmets to the gust of fetid wind.

The command was given again and the second line

fired. The concentrated shot had the bearboon roaring in pain, its helmeted head thrown back, blinking to remove the hot lead from its now-watering eyes.

The command sounded a third time. Count Rostov was getting into giant killing; he could already see his medal. The following wave of shot sent Gruber crashing backwards against a well-formed wall that creaked and buckled but, in a salute to Russian architects, did not give. Rostov gave yet another command to fire, and it was then that his lack of real military experience shone through. He had given no command to reload, so all lines of fire were spent. They had been good soldiers and followed the commands to the letter, exactly as their training had taught them.

'Not to worry,' shouted Rostov. 'All ranks reload!'

It is a test that very few soldiers have to go through, but … under pressure from a rampaging monster, can you reload a ball-firing musket? It involves pushing the right amount of wadding into your gun, biting the top off your ammo pouch and pouring the shot down the barrel, before priming your firing pan with gunpowder.

All this activity was being undertaken while a 30-foot-tall giant bear/baboon creature tore flagpoles from the ground in one sweep of its massive arm. It then gathered the concrete-encrusted poles together in a single hand, crudely constructing a huge multi-headed club, which it swung around, aiming for the squad of musketeers.

The makeshift club took the group of men out like a baseball bat arcing through a chocolate cake. Some exploded with the impact, some fell where they were stood and most of the back line flew through the air, either to impact with the surrounding buildings or to sail out into the middle of the river Moskva. Very few managed to get a second shot at the monster.

Gruber held the club in both hands above his head and pumped the air. A big grin crossed Tripps' face as, 1,500 miles away, he too pumped the air in celebration.

Word went out around the globe about the attack on Moscow, and in a hotel in Berlin, while eating a late breakfast, Iron was informed of it by an excited bellhop who thought, but was not quite a hundred percent sure, that this meant that Germany was going to war with Russia.

Iron turned to see several people talking in excited huddles. The word 'monster' was being said with all too much frequency for Iron. Hadn't he just joined a secret organisation whose purpose it was to make people believe there were no monsters? He certainly didn't want this ride to end so soon.

So he wiped his mouth on a napkin and hurried to his room. On arriving, he found a disgruntled maid trying to clean away the bits of straw matting and plaster dust that covered everything. He hurried her out, pushing either an obscene or insulting amount of money into her hand – he had no idea on the local currency. Then he quickly suited up.

In his head it felt like a lightning change, but in fact, some of the connections were tricky and it took him probably half an hour before he was ready. But eventually, in a posh room of a Berlin hotel, Iron stood armour-clad. It was only then that he remembered the vast distance between Berlin and Moscow. He thought that Poland might actually be in the way.

'Damn it' he sighed. What good was it to be able to

dress as a knight to fight dragons, only to find you couldn't get to them? Oh for a trusty steed.

Iron guessed there must be at least one more agent in Moscow to deal with the situation, so even if he caught the train, it would be all over before he arrived. He fiddled with the switches on his chest. Maybe one would tune him into a Moscow agent's radio and he could at least hear the battle played out.

The third switch he tried initiated a roaring noise, and without warning, Iron shot through the open balcony doors into the Berlin sky, screaming the entire time.

9
MEETINGS

Rasputin liked the courage of this new nanny, but he had come to realise that British nannies seemed to be made of different stuff from the rest of the world's women. They took no nonsense and rarely gave any. They could bring a child or a king from full blown ranting anger to apologetic shyness with just a look, and they had more practical knowledge in one fingertip than a whole household of staff had between them.

The monk and the nanny walked into the forest, and around them, the trees thinned to reveal a clearing. And there, in the clearing, was the creature.

Beatrix had read many books on animals, and despite its size and wings, she was pretty sure this was either a mandrill or a baboon. However, whatever it was didn't look too happy.

Peter had realised too late that Gruber's plan was going to be in operation long before his and, although he was less than an hour old, he felt intense rivalry toward his monkey-o-matic brother. He had decided to find a good Russian citizen and therefore follow his master's command precisely, proving his solidarity to the cause and hopefully creating a better monster in the process.

All he had found so far was a coach and horses that moved too fast, and now a girl who was about as Russian as Peter was human. The baboon had no time for silly girls, so he bared his teeth and rushed in to the attack. He certainly didn't expect a strange-looking bearded fellow to appear as if from nowhere so that rather than his hooked fingers finding the soft flesh of a lady, they instead tore at the knotted muscles of an old monk.

Rasputin howled in pain and a series of curse words exited his mouth with such fluid rapidity it stopped Peter in his tracks.

Nuts! thought the winged primate. *I find a typical Russian and I practically gut him!*

He approached the prone, writhing form of the man, hoping that there was at least something he could salvage from this mess, when an umbrella, which felt surprisingly like an ancient mace, was brought down hard on his head.

He went cross-eyed for a brief second and then collapsed in an unattractive heap of fur, muscle and claw.

Beatrix rushed to the cursing monk and gave him a look that made every word taste like soap. Looking around, she spotted what looked like a bottle of beer or perhaps mead. She was sure that the baboon hadn't been carrying it and therefore it must have fallen from Rasputin's robes. She picked it up and uncorked it. The monk seemed to be in pain still, and she thought that perhaps a medicinal draught would help, so she pushed it to his lips. He took the bottle and drank.

It is true, he thought. *Nannies do always have the*

correct medicine for the job. He could already feel a healing warmth spreading through his frame.

Nanny Honey told him to stay where he was and headed back to the coach. She was surprised to find the driver talking excitedly to the driver of a carriage going the other way.

On seeing Beatrix he shouted in Russian, 'I told you it was monsters! That creature must have been a baby, as the daddy is attacking Moscow as we speak. They've been sent by the Germans.'

It has started then, thought Bea. But right now she had more pressing matters.

'Never mind that! The monk has been hurt in the woods and we need to get him back to the palace before he dies.'

After explaining all to his counterpart in the other carriage, who set off at sped back to Moscow, Bea's driver followed her back into the forest to bring the injured mystic to safety and medical help.

The two of them ignored the immobile body of the winged baboon-thing. Taking an end each, they carried the smiling monk to safety. The entire time, the driver babbled on about the monster attack on Moscow and the army being unable to do a thing. As they loaded the now singing monk into the coach, Bea unhooked her bike. She wondered what the drink had been – obviously it was fairly potent.

'Get him to the Palace,' she instructed the driver. 'I will ride on to Saint Petersburg and send for a surgeon. His abdomen is very badly damaged and I doubt the Palace physicians will have the right equipment.'

She hoisted her skirts and mounted the bike, fully aware that Mother wouldn't approve, before riding off at speed while the driver turned the carriage in the road.

She would get to Saint Petersburg and then she planned to catch a train to Moscow. With any luck, she could help defeat the beast and hopefully stop any rumours getting out to the rest of Russia.

It was always surprisingly easy to cover a monster story with a more plausible one, but only if you got the monster bagged and tagged quickly enough. Pictures in the press wouldn't do at all, especially as the Russians were already pointing fingers at the Germans.

High up in the clouds, Iron was having the best fun he'd had in his life.

Simple movements of his body created the most giddying acrobatics but he felt so comfortable, it was as if he were weightless. He would reach Moscow in just an hour, he was sure of it, and that was when the true heroics would begin.

An aerial battle against a giant monster! He couldn't wait! Books would be written about him, possibly, although names would have to be changed due to the Order's guidelines.

Eventually he emerged from the cloud cover, and in the distance he could see Moscow. He could also see, even from here, that something big was moving through the city.

Bea was efficiently running through a possible checklist of ways to defeat a 30 foot monster. She had completed her tasks in Saint Petersburg and was now *en route* for Moscow by train. Her contemplations were broken by commotion elsewhere in the carriage. People had rushed to the windows on the other side and were talking excitedly.

'It's one of ours! I knew they wouldn't let Moscow fall,' a voice said.

Bea moved over to the opposite window and looked out. She had a view of the rolling fields on the outskirts of Moscow. And in the fields stood Russia's possible salvation from the invading German giant.

A monster they could call their own.

It stood around 40 foot tall and definitely had something of rural Russia about it. It walked upright like a man, but everything else suggested donkey or possibly mule. It had a bulbous belly and was covered in thick, dark hair. Its legs were awkward-looking, with the backward shape familiar to the legs of donkeys, however they seemed most odd when supporting a upright body.

Its arms were strongly-muscled, finished in a peculiar hand-hoof combination that definitely wasn't the product of careful evolution. Its ears were long, hanging down like those of a lop-eared rabbit, and it had a long black mane and thick facial hair that looked just like a beard.

Bea blinked. She recognised it. She looked again and whispered 'Rasputin' to herself before hurriedly returning to her seat to think.

Gruber, controlled by Tripps, had been having a fun time destroying Moscow until around a half hour earlier. With the birth of the second Kaiju, Tripps had lost control of them both. High in his *Arc*, he cursed his oversight. It was hard enough controlling his own thoughts and the actions of one monster, let alone two. Well it was a lesson learnt, and he knew he had two perfectly good baboons in the field to guide the two creatures' actions near enough to his wishes.

Without the controlling influence of the doctor, Gruber had become bored, and was now sitting in Red Square scratching his fur and looking around in a very baboon-like manner.

Around him, the carnage was great. Many Russians had lost their lives to the marauding monster, and some of the buildings had been crushed. However, many of the older dwellings had withstood the creature's passage – testament to good Russian building techniques. The army was lurking in every available street, all waiting to open fire the moment the monster moved, but after a day of ineffectual conflict no-one was particularly eager to engage the beast again.

Suddenly Gruber stopped scratching and stretched, sniffing the air. Every gun trained on the creature moved with it as it shifted, and not one breath was taken by the surrounding soldiers. Then, it was gone. The bearboon moved like lightning, and guns opened fire from everywhere, but the creature was so quick that most bullets just tore plaster from the buildings or smashed the glass in the surrounding windows.

The Berlin bear hurdled and climbed through the towers of the Kremlin and was off into the wilds beyond the city. Russian Generals shouted orders and, as quickly as they dared, gave chase. All eyes however went upwards, as a small, noisy shape streaked through the sky after the disappearing monster.

Iron was shocked at how big the creature was, and even more shocked that it was running away. He had no idea how much fuel he had left and was suddenly aware that he could have a long walk back to Berlin and the rest of his stuff. He was trying to think of his rules of engagement and remembered that he still hadn't found the time to read the Royal Order of Dragons' documents. Cursing himself, he continued to give chase, convincing himself that he would be fine if he just made it up as he went along.

The train came to a stop in the middle of nowhere. Someone had pulled the emergency cord, and the driver had been only too happy to stop.

As everyone looked out of the far side of the train, Beatrix Honey made her way to the luggage compartment, and disembarked on the near side taking her bike with her. She made her way up to the nearest roadway and gave chase after the monster.

It was as she crested a rise that she saw, coming at her from the other direction, another monster of almost equal size, with the distinctive loping gait of one of the large apes.

The two creatures slammed into each other with earth-rocking force. The mule-thing – Rasputin as Bea considered him to be – was still coming downhill and hadn't stopped his charge since he had set off. As a force of nature he was almost unstoppable. The bearboon on the other hand was at a disadvantage: he was heading uphill. The creature stopped, and braced himself for the impact.

The results were spectacular. The bearboon was taken clean off his feet by the mule's stampede, and with an inability to grab his opponent, he flew through the air before coming to a rest in a copse of trees, which exploded into splinters or were torn out by their ancient roots as the monster ploughed through them.

The mule let out a deafening bray of victory,

although his hand briefly touched the area where only recently as a human he had been so badly wounded. The bearboon was up and on his feet again in seconds, but fatigue from his rampaging around Moscow was starting to show. The Berlin bear reached into the jumble of fallen trees and selected two mighty trunks. Now armed, his confidence grew and he stalked the mule like a prize-fighter.

The mule had always liked a bar fight; or at least the part of his memory that was Rasputin's told him so, and was glad his opponent and chosen to battle with weapons. Folks with weapons always got a bit too focused on them and missed out on the more natural and unsuspected attack.

For a while the two enormous monsters paced around each other, the bear throwing the odd strike out with a tree, judging distance. Then, without warning, the mule sprang. The impact took both creatures off their feet, and large chunks of countryside tore away as they rolled together. The Moscow mule used hid hoof hands to great effect, knocking the now seemingly ridiculous helmet off the bearboon's head, allowing hard blows to fall on a cranium that cracked with every impact.

Gruber was helpless. His extended weapons were no good at close quarters but, as Rasputin had anticipated, he did not let them go. A hard strike to the jaw and the bear became motionless.

His eyes glazed, and he crashed to the ground with an enormous thud that could be heard as far away as Moscow. Beatrice fell from her bike as the ground shook, and she disentangled herself from it as quickly as she could.

The mule rolled his opponent away and reared up to bring his hard hooves down in a devastating blow, but he was stopped short. From out of nowhere a flying man appeared. He approached fast, and suddenly smaller objects hit the mule's body with such force and rapidity, that every tiny impact pushed him back and felt like a sledgehammer. Slowly the creature sank to his knees.

Bea ran forward. She certainly had seen no redeemable features in the strange mystic but his death would most certainly be the undoing of young Alexi's life, and as a NANI agent she had sworn to protect the young Tsar. She skidded to a halt, realising too late that the giant beast that had been Rasputin was toppling over … and she was right beneath him!

Iron saw a girl in maroon and purple run forward, and he realised that she was about to be crushed by the falling beast. He stopped firing and swooped beneath the creature's tumbling body, snatching her from harm's way as the great weight slammed home into the soft earth.

He couldn't help but grin at her beautiful face, even though he was hidden beneath the helmet. This was certainly not Cotton in his arms. He had killed the monster and saved the maiden. There wouldn't just be stories, there would be legends, possibly romance. So he was certainly surprised when she slapped his chest and called him an idiot.

Landing, he placed her down before him, suddenly happy that the helmet was hiding his face, as he was blushing terribly.

'You shot the wrong one,' berated the woman. 'That's Rasputin! He was protecting Russia.'

Iron turned and looked at the two fallen monsters

behind him. When he turned back, he found the girl looking him intently up and down.

'What are you supposed to be, anyway?'

Iron was even more hurt and couldn't help breaking the first rule.

'I'm Lord Branding of the Royal Order of Dragons. We have sworn to protect the world against monsters.' He pointed a gauntleted hand back at the fallen creatures. 'And unless I'm much mistaken, those are monsters.' He paused, 'Also, from what I've heard, if that is Grigori Rasputin, then whether he's a giant donkey or not he will always be a monster.'

Bea couldn't fault the knight's logic. They *had* both been monsters, and hadn't Nana told her not to look too much further than Rasputin? In all honesty she was cross because this flying tin can had stolen her thunder.

She narrowed her eyes at him and saluted. 'Miss Beatrix Honey, agent of NANI.' She smiled disarmingly as she lowered her salute. 'My mission is to prevent a world war, and these big beasties seem determined to make it happen.' She looked over at the bodies. 'Where has he gone?' she said.

Iron looked back, but the Moscow mule was nowhere to be seen.

Beatrix and Iron hurried over to the trench that the monster had made with its fall. At the bottom was the body of the monk, naked and groaning in the mud. Bea reached into her travel bag and pulled free a tartan blanket, of great enough size to cover Rasputin like a robe.

'The army will be here soon,' said Iron. 'I've no doubt of that. I flew over them on the way. You'd best get that fellow somewhere safe and looked after and I will try to come up with a story to explain the other …

thing … monster … bear.'

'Where can I find you?' said Beatrix, aware she had never asked to find anyone before as she had always been happy doing things on her own.

Iron hated what he had to do next, as he rather liked the girl.

'You can't, I'm afraid. If I'm needed, I'll find you.'

There was a long pause as Bea looked at Iron's eyes through the helmet goggles.

'Really? That's your best line?' she laughed. 'Well good luck with that, I have a world war to stop. If, however, *you* need *me*, I'm a nanny at the Romanov residence.'

She helped Rasputin to his feet, and together they staggered out of the trench and back toward the train. Iron wanted to stop her and point out that he was new to all this, but he heard the sounds of the army approaching and decided he had better get on with the job of distracting them.

10
PURSUIT

Iron approached them, gently waving both hands above his head and trying to look as unthreatening as possible. The troops were mainly mounted on horses and quite clearly hadn't arrived as quickly as they might have done. Iron had a feeling that they weren't too enthusiastic to meet the two massive monsters that had been doing battle.

The mass of men slowed and two officers rode out to meet Iron. They were fairly certain that this was the man who had flown over their heads earlier in pursuit of the beast and should, therefore, be treated as an ally. Especially as he seemed to have killed it. Iron saluted and received a salute back before one of the officers addressed him in Russian.

'Вы разрушили существо?'

Iron held up his hands. 'I'm sorry, I'm afraid I don't speak Russian. I was just travelling past and thought I'd lend a hand.'

The officer paused, and then said again, in perfect accented English:

'Have you destroyed the creature?'

The Russian craned his neck to look at the fallen beast, and Iron also turned to look at the foe. It did most certainly look very dead, lying prone on the ground with its tongue hanging out.

'I wouldn't say destroyed,' Iron mused. 'Its chest is still rising and falling, so it's not even dead. It does however appear to be out for the count.'

'We should make sure it's dead. The last thing I want my men to be doing is fighting that creature again.'

As if that had been its cue, the bearboon stirred and shook its massive head. It struggled to its feet. The horses were startled and reared up, flinging the officers from their mounts. The wounded bearboon looked around, and ran for open country. Behind it, some of the startled soldiers started firing erratically at its fleeing form.

Iron couldn't believe his eyes. He swiftly flicked a switch on his control panel, ready to give chase, but nothing happened apart from a soft, steady clicking. He flicked the switch a couple more times, and sighed. The creature was escaping fast, so Iron took the only option left open to him. He grabbed one of the horses, leaped into its saddle, and kicked it into movement.

Trained for war, the chestnut mare was happy to follow commands, even though they drove it at a gallop after the bear creature. Not wanting to risk finding a non-working weapon upon catching and engaging the beast, Iron tried a test shot and took out a harmless tree as he rode by. He remembered the nanny's words and was suddenly aware that maybe dispatching the creature wasn't the best course of action but instead following it back to its lair would a better use of his time. Besides, he would always have the option to take it down should the need arise.

Tripps was back in control of the bearboon. The moment Rasputin had shaken off the cocktail and returned to normal, the doctor had come back on line. He had spent the last few minutes trying to rouse his creature and get it to an area of safety. He was aiming for the largest body of water he could locate. At first he had no idea what had been happening with his Kaiju since he had lost control, but as he manipulated the mind of the beast, slowly the memories of the Berlin bear trickled into his own head.

So what had happened to the Moscow mule? One moment it was there, about to administer a killing blow, and then it had gone. The creatures may have been built for causing destruction but Tripps didn't want them destroyed, not before they reached their full potential.

Iron galloped after the only Kaiju still moving around. The bearboon made light work of the countryside. Trees were smashed out of its way or simply jumped over. Hedges were crushed and mangled, and homesteads were destroyed like matchwood. Iron, however, had to avoid the devastation and obstacles in his path. Surprisingly he managed to keep up and, to be honest, it wasn't difficult to keep track of something that towered above the landscape.

The light was starting to fade as they crested a hill to see, on the other side, the magnificent Lake Llmen. The creature was most certainly heading for its cool dark waters, but in front of it was a small village, lights glowing as dusk fell.

The place was obvious to Iron and was also right in the monster's path. If the destruction so far was anything to go by, the village didn't stand a chance. Iron aimed his wrist-mounted gun and opened fire.

Tripps felt no pain from the metal balls that tore into the creature but he was aware that he was being attacked. He stopped the bearboon and made it turn to see its attacker. One man on a horse? Was that all? Like a Don Quixote tilting at windmills. Tripps didn't have time for heroes: he never saw the point of them.

Iron reined his horse in. He had most certainly got the creature's full attention. He swallowed. This was good for the village but not so good for him. He had no shots left in the weapon and, from his earlier experience, was quite certain he could no longer fly. The bearboon charged back toward him, roaring ferociously as it came. Turning the horse, Iron galloped hard away, leading the beast around the village rather than through it.

He jumped a fence and was suddenly in the middle of a herd of cows that scattered in slow motion as the horse moved through them. Leaping the far fence and leaving them behind, he steered back toward the lake.

Iron knew he couldn't challenge the creature with no weapons but reasoned that if it saw the water it had been heading for, it might leave him be and the village would be saved. There was a sudden commotion behind him, and Iron looked back to see a cow sail rapidly up behind him before soaring over his head and bouncing along the ground in front of him. Another cow quickly flew overhead, bounced once and splashed into the lake. The beast was throwing the cattle like stones. It was already grasping two more startled, struggling beasts from the field and, like a trained cricketer, pitched one straight at Iron and his mount.

They were, luckily, moving fast, and where they had been wasn't where they were, as the cow flew past. It went in low and as it hit the lake it skimmed. One, two, three bounces off the water before it hit the surface again and sank. Moments later it bobbed back up, startled, legs kicking itself back to the shore.

Iron had watched the spectacle of flying cows, and taken his mind off his own mount too long. He had not only slowed but had ridden in a straight line, so the next cow hit his horse with such force they were all knocked to the ground in a heap.

Iron scrabbled free of the fallen horse as it kicked its legs alarmingly, the metal-shod hooves narrowly missing his head as he tried to avoid the cow that was also struggling to get back to its feet. He crawled away as fast as he could but he could feel, even in the approaching darkness of the night, the growing shadow of his enemy. He rolled onto his back just as a colossal paw came crushing down on him.

Deep inside the beast, Gruber felt the small human squish beneath his foot. He experienced a rush of pleasure at having successfully defeated his enemy, and without another care, jumped with a huge splash into the lake. He was happy to let the mind of the doctor control him as they swam further out into the cool, enveloping waters. He could easily wait here, out in the depths, undetected until the doctor needed him again. There were plenty of fish to eat and even some cows … It was a good place to hide.

11
ARC IN THE CLOUDS

Having ridden the train with the injured Rasputin back to Saint Petersburg (she claimed he had been drinking if anyone offered words of concern for her companion), Beatrix got him to a hospital where he was treated immediately for his injuries. Claiming that she was the nanny for his family neatly avoided any further questions (and was only a slight diversion from the truth), and she was even offered a room in the hospital for the night. She politely declined, explaining that she had a bike and that she should really get back to the children as they worried so.

Rasputin was in good hands and would recover. They had concocted some story about him being attacked by a disgruntled woman. All the doctors and nurses had believed that without question and patched up the monk as quickly as they could, more out of respect for the Royal Family than any loyalty to Rasputin himself.

As Bea rode her bicycle along the dark roads back to the Palace, she kept her eye out for the wooded area where the initial attack had taken place. She realised that she had gone a little too far when she arrived at the splintered remains of the coach and what she could only assume had once been the horses and driver. She grimaced at the slaughter and wondered if she was doing the right thing. But she had to know.

Slowly retracing her steps, she headed into the trees, the handy removable lantern from her bike lighting the way. Eventually she found the clearing. Rasputin's blood was splashed across the place, but she could see signs in the leaves and dirt that something had dragged itself toward a hollow log. She approached carefully and shone the lantern inside and there, curled up, was the winged baboon. She grabbed one of its legs and pulled the primate free from its hiding place.

Instantly the creature awoke and struggled, fangs bared, ready to fight. Then it saw the umbrella held threateningly in Nanny Honey's hand, and quickly became calm and slightly subdued. It had no wish to be clocked around the head again.

'Ah! We understand each other,' said Beatrix, using her very best calm but scolding voice.

The baboon did little more than raise its hand to the still tender lump on its head, and Beatrix smiled.

'Now, I know it's not polite to shoot the messenger, but that doesn't mean you can't soften one up until it decides to take you to the message writer.' She tapped the handle of her umbrella against her gloved hand.

Baboons are strange animals. In the wild they run in packs led by the most aggressive, an instinct that has done the troops of baboons on the savannah a great service through the years, as they needed to survive against so many other predators. Peter was less than a day old and had no pack. Here, however, was an alpha female, who had, as far as Peter was concerned, done everything with aggression, and every instinct in his baboon brain wanted to obey her.

If only he could work out what it was she wanted, apart from to hit him again. Of course he knew a way of finding out exactly what she wanted, but it would mean sliding on the little crown again, and the crowns were all back at the flying ship.

Peter jumped up and pointed to the sky, flapping his wings to lift him off the ground and flexing his strong prehensile toes.

'You want to fly me somewhere?' Bea asked. 'Well I admit I saw someone else do it earlier today and it looked like fun.' She waved the umbrella, making Peter flinch. 'And I haven't got the hang of this thing yet.'

Peter looked at the night sky and covered his eyes.

'Oh! I see, we need to wait until morning?'

She patted the ape on the head. He cringed and she smiled gently. 'I'll see you tomorrow then,' she said, before walking away back to her bike.

Re-hooking the lantern, she set off once again, and eventually arrived back at the Palace. It was nice to return to the friendly face of Nana, who had steaming mugs of tea waiting and an eager desire for a conversation about the day. Already it seemed stories were warping. Few were talking of monsters, but all were talking of Germany's attack on Moscow. Beatrix listened, smiled, and nodded at the right places, but her mind was on what new adventure the next day would bring.

Early the next morning, Beatrix got herself ready before setting off again on her trusty bike to the forest and the waiting baboon.

When she got there, the creature looked more

impatient than any of the children ever entrusted to Nanny Honey. She had brought him fresh fruit from the kitchen and sat quietly while he ate. Even so, she kept her umbrella close to hand and in plain sight so that her simian companion would realise that the fruit was an act of fuelling up her ride and not a sign of weakness.

As soon as the monkey was fed, he stretched and tested his wings. They seemed strong. Bea didn't expect the flight to be pleasant or warm so she had dressed well for the journey. Buttoning her coat tight and adjusting the pins in her hat, she placed a small pair of cinder goggles across her eyes to stop them from watering and wrapped her chiffon scarf around the exposed regions of her face, before signalling that she was ready.

The large baboon moved behind her and in one leap was on her back. The sudden weight made Beatrix stoop, but she gained her footing and stood upright.

'No signs of weakness girl,' she said, more to herself than to the baboon.

The creature on her back tensed, and they were suddenly airborne.

The sensation was magnificent. The baboon felt the same as any tight-fitting back pack, once its weight had been taken off her legs. It had wrapped its strong arms around hers and hooked its toes in the belt of her maroon coat, allowing Bea complete freedom of movement. After a while she had nearly forgotten about the baboon entirely and the flapping wings felt like her own, taking her up and away to her destination, whatever or wherever that might be.

They skimmed through cold, wet clouds before emerging glistening and fresh into the bright blue sky. The sun dried them, and all the time, the baboon kept moving them forward. It was exciting and exhilarating.

After a time, something came into view in the distance, and Bea squinted through her goggles to make it out. From a distance it looked more like a giant floating teapot than anything else, but as they came closer, Bea could see that it was like a ship suspended beneath a vast balloon. Where a figurehead might have traditionally been, instead there was a large spout-like funnel made from some metallic substance.

The large, rounded body of the hull was peppered with portholes and windows, and the flat deck had what appeared to be a church or maybe a chapel built upon it. In front of that was a wheelhouse that overlooked an impressive gun emplacement bristling with barrels. As they drew closer, Bea's nerves began to flutter. She had no idea who could possibly be living on a strange vessel like this, but whoever it was, she was sure that they wished to start a war that would consume the globe.

The teapot-shaped airship and world destruction suddenly felt like unpleasant bedfellows. Bea frowned. It was like finding out that your grandparents were in fact grave robbers.

The baboon and Nanny Honey flew around the deck and landed. The creature released Bea, and hopped down. It was exhausted and sidled off to sit quietly in a corner by the wheelhouse. Beatrice checked that they were alone, took her umbrella from where it had been secured in the handles of her travel bag, and quietly crept around the deck, looking in all the windows.

For the most part, this incredible construction resembled a boat inside as it did outside: charts and compasses were laid out on tables while hooks on the walls were hung with faded waterproof coats and hats. Through the window of the chapel-like building she saw a home that would be comfortable on any English estate.

It had warm oak panels around the walls, and crafted bookshelves full of leather-bound volumes. The rugs looked deep and plush and pictures by a skilful artist graced every wall. No-one seemed to be around, but she felt it unlikely that they had popped out for a packet of biscuits, so she carried on making her way around the ship, checking in every window she passed.

At one porthole, she had to blink and look twice. The room beyond was a bedroom, looking very much like every woman's dream room, all except for the bed. This appeared to be like any ordinary piece of furniture at first glance, but on closer inspection, Bea realised that it was actually a large tank full of clean water, and drifting just below the surface was a mermaid. She had soft, glistening skin from the waist up and rainbow-coloured scales from the waist down. Her eyes were tightly shut and her hair, the softest green, drifted lazily about her body, covering her modesty whichever way she moved in the water.

As Beatrix gazed at her, an alarm rang beside the bed. It was an intricate device, on which two tiny sculpted mermen turned to strike a bell with tridents held in their hands. The mermaid's eyes opened and she drifted up to the surface, reached out and over to the alarm and silenced the chimes.

The mermaid stretched. Beside the bed was another glass tank. This one was shaped like a bell, but with the opening in the domed top instead of at the bottom. Raising herself from the tank on the bed, the mermaid lowered herself into the bell so that it fit her like a skirt.

Bea watched as she flicked her tail across a selection of levers set into the tank's base, and the whole contraption glided over to a dressing table. The mermaid lightly towelled her upper body dry and brushed her pale green hair before sliding on a blouse. She efficiently styled her hair into the shape of an octopus and applied the subtlest of make-up to her perfect features. Finally she wrapped a swathe of fabric around the tank, covering her fish tail and thus giving her the look of someone wearing a full crinoline skirt, before she fastened a corset over the whole ensemble. If you didn't know, you would believe she was nothing more than a society lady in her finest clothes.

Bea had remained transfixed the entire time, some part of her wishing that she was the graceful women in the water, until a slight buzz-like cough drew her attention.

She turned and saw, standing beside her, a monster from the depths of hell. It was part-monkey, but with the hideous head of a gigantic house fly.

A door opened alongside, and the mermaid emerged. She held a wicked-looking cutlass in her hand, and moved it to point at the hapless nanny. Bea swallowed. She suddenly felt very human, and very alone.

12
FLASHING BLADES

Igor didn't take well to intruders, especially voyeuristic ones who looked through her bedroom window, and therefore she hadn't come on deck simply to ask questions. Sabre drawn, she approached the woman purposefully and thrust straight for the intruder's chest, but her blade was parried aside by an umbrella.

Bea was already in a fencing stance, her umbrella held as professionally as any swordsman's weapon. The umbrella tip looked particularly flat and sharp, and as deadly as the smile on Bea's face. Igor smiled back and Flyn disappeared out of harm's way as the two women paced around each other looking for the best attack position.

In lightning-fast movements their weapons clashed to one side then the other, before Bea's bladed umbrella swished gracefully toward Igor's face. The mermaid simply leaned back slightly and it whistled by.

The smiles didn't leave either woman's face, and they paced slowly around each other in the opposite direction, like caged tigresses. Weapons struck again, one, two, and Igor's blade slipped harmlessly past Bea's defence as the nanny turned to avoid a hit with the tiniest of movements.

The smiles widened and the stances returned. Bea pushed her advantage, delivering a quick striking of blows. Igor was forced to retreat onto the wider deck as first one, then a second and then a third blow had to be parried.

The fourth swish saw the mermaid in a better position and her parries became fiercer, so Bea gave up ground in the next couple of blows. Soon the two obviously adept fighters were trading blows with lightning keenness and precision. The familiar sound of metal on metal rang across the clouds as the two pushed backwards and forwards, each thrust met with a parry or turned to an advantage, but neither gaining the upper hand.

Blades went low and high, came in fast from every side, and every time they were predicted by the other. Bea's stance had the elegant manner of a Spanish fighter and her weapon lost nothing in its unconventional appearance against the cutlass of her opponent. Igor's gliding motion made her every move appear effortless in its simplicity.

Bea could only admire the prowess of the woman who, beneath her skirts, was like a swan, a flurry of tail movement operating levers to make her tank dance across the deck and put her in just the right position every time to parry or thrust her blade.

Bea spun as if she had overstepped her line, but the graceful arc of her umbrella just soared around and came fast up on the unprotected side of the mermaid, who again with agile reflexes moved herself to parry the blow. Then they resumed their rhythmic dance in front of the gun emplacement and around its side, as some of the simian crew started to appear on the deck to watch the spectacle unfold.

Peter the baboon simply couldn't understand whether there was an attempt being made for the Alpha female position or whether some unknown courtship dance was underway. Whichever it might be, he sensibly chose to stay out of the way. The nanny now seemed to have the advantage, as Igor was pushed by a series of blows up a ridged slope to the higher deck behind the large gun.

'You seem very agile for a fish out of water,' Bea teased, hoping to break the mermaid's concentration while keeping her attention focused on the flurry of blows that slowly pushed her tank back toward a short drop down, which would surely tip her out and across the deck if she fell.

'And you seem very overconfident for a mammal so fresh out of the trees,' said Igor, gently jumping backwards, tank and all, off the drop and landing squarely on the lower deck.

Bea saw an advantage and, grabbing her umbrella before her in both hands, used it like a gymnastics bar, to flip over the mermaid's head and land behind her on the deck, making a strike for her unprotected back.

But the mermaid had her in sight the entire time and performed a simple spin on the spot as Bea flew over her head, and their blades met again with a musical ting. Then Igor had the advantage, pushing Beatrix back toward the wall of the wheelhouse, sending ape-like LUMPs flying aside like a small flurry of seagulls.

'You are so fast,' remarked Bea, more with

admiration than worry.

'Thank you. I find not having the drag of water against my limbs is an advantage; one from which you will unfortunately not benefit.'

With this, Bea's back was forced against the wheelhouse wall, and she was certainly at a disadvantage in this position.

'I admit you do seem to be less hampered by drag factor, but I can always do this ...'

Bea pressed a small recessed button in the carved hare handle of her umbrella, just as Igor thrust, and the umbrella part of her weapon opened up, almost like a shield. The blade of the cutlass went through the strong fabric and snared, coming to a stop only an inch from Bea's soft throat.

With a chuckle, Bea spun the umbrella canopy. The weapon was torn from Igor's hand and spun through the air, halting like a javelin buried deep in the wooden keel of the *Arc*. Another press of the button and the umbrella snapped shut.. Igor, now hopelessly weaponless, was at the mercy of the nanny's blade.

'Seems not wanting to get wet has given the advantage to me,' Bea said with a grin. 'So, any last words?'

Igor smiled, hair turning turquoise. 'Only two. Surf's up!' And with this she flipped from her tank, which went spinning across the deck like a dervish, colourful skirts flying up all around it. Like a salmon, she had leapt into the air, and for a moment, all Bea could see was the magnificent glistening glint of her rainbow-scale tail before the powerful limb slapped its fan-like fins across her face.

Bea was thrown so far across the deck that she spun over the *Arc*'s side. Only by the quickness of her training did she prevent herself from plummeting down through the clouds, as her booted toes hooked her onto the deck. However, now she was upside down, skirts around her ears, flashing her bloomers to a deck full of peering monkeys.

Igor spiralled gracefully through the air in a back flip and landed back in her tank with not so much as a ripple. She glided to her cutlass and with some effort pulled it free of the wood. Bea pushed herself hard off the bulkhead she now faced and managed to hook her umbrella around one of the supports. She pulled, and like Nosferatu, rose back above the deck.

She still wasn't out of danger, so she turned on her heels until she faced inwards, opening her umbrella to allow the gentle wind to carry her one step forward and back onto the deck once more.

Igor pressed her advantage, disarmed the nanny of her umbrella in one strike to the handle, and in a swift movement brought the point of her cutlass up underneath Bea's chin. Bea gulped. Before her was an armed mermaid with the advantage and a certain desire to want her off the flying boat, and behind her was a fall of many miles to the ground.

Bea saw the muscles in Igor's arm tense as her hair turned blood red, like a viper about to strike, and she closed her eyes tightly in anticipation.

'Stop!'

The voice was calm, deep, English and authoritative. Bea opened one eye and saw the figure of the man who had spoken.

He stood in a tailored jacket of fine blue, with white piping lining the cuffs and collar. His trousers were white and tucked into black knee-high boots polished to shine like mirrors. His handlebar moustache had turned snow white over time and his glasses were round and rose-tinted. The glass dome that was his cranium held the unsettling sight of his exposed brain, around which two small fish were darting, nibbling at it to keep it clean and fresh.

The man walked up alongside Igor, whose strike hadn't come but whose blade also hadn't lowered.

'Good morning, my sweet sea shanty. I see you are up and have found yourself some morning exercise on deck.' The squat figure of the ape-fly edged out from behind the doctor as he spoke. 'It seems a shame to throw a specimen back that obviously came a long way to see us.'

He placed a hand on Igor's and lowered her blade slightly.

'I think, considering the mission we have set ourselves upon, we should maybe find out if our guest is working alone or if we should man the guns and break out the flying gorillas.'

He looked at Bea through the rose glass of his eyewear. 'I'm sure you'd be happy to tell us your tale, wouldn't you my dear? Or should we drop you off somewhere?'

Beatrix had never truly had to deal with madness that masqueraded so well as acceptable behaviour, and in all honesty she doubted she had ever been this scared.

'My name is Dr Horatio Tripps, my dear. Please come this way.'

The man bowed slightly, and Bea was ushered before him to one of the doors into the flying ship. She had no choice but to comply.

Soon, Dr Tripps was sat opposite Beatrix in his study. He was in his high-backed leather Captain's chair, drinking a fresh cup of morning tea and spreading homemade marmalade on his toast as Igor stood broodingly behind him. Her cutlass was now sheathed in a scabbard at her hip.

Bea had no tea or toast but instead brass clamps held her securely to the chair, at her ankles, wrist, waist and forehead. The chair was made from wood but she had been provided with a cushion for comfort. It's the little details that single out a madman.

She had been quite forward about who she was and why she was here. She spoke about acting alone but being part of a bigger network. She spoke of the horror of what he was doing, and the need to find out why and if possible to stop him. She added that she hadn't intended this request to be by the blade or any other form of attack but instead by reasoned debate, appealing to his instincts regarding what was right.

His laughter, of about a minute's duration, had assured her that she had taken the wrong course of action and she should have just flown up and cut the balloon free.

Now it was the doctor's turn to speak, for he had been asked a question, several in fact, in the course of her explanation.

'My name, as you know, is Dr Horatio Tripps. Twelve years ago I was at the Royal Society in London when I had the fortune to see a demonstration of the first diesel engine. While my fellow scientists and the slack-jawed simpletons of the press looked on with adoration and awe, I was the only one who saw any sense, for I was filled with a creeping chill of horror.'

He took a bite of toast and a long sip of tea to wash it down.

'I am aware that the British Empire did not create

the wonders of steam, but we did seize instantly upon its advantages, and with it we built vast ships and continent-spanning railways. We made the globe a lot smaller and opened it up for proper conquest and unity under one flag. Can't say the other burgeoning Empires weren't a bit peeved, and many wished they had thought of it first. By a stroke of luck it had fallen into the hands of the good guys, and the world was heading toward being a happier place.'

He finished his toast and gazed out of the porthole wistfully for a while before continuing.

'When I saw this device invented by a Frenchman, raised as a German, I realised instantly we might not get first dibs on its usage. The advantage would move from steam countries to diesel countries, and many of those, as history has told us time and time again, are the bad guys. I vowed then that I would use my skills to build a threat that would drive anyone using diesel away from it. At first I was going to attack the countries that used diesel, but so many turned to it that I soon realised I must make them attack each other and thus come to their own conclusion that they became more aggressive under its sway. War seems the only way to make the world see the monumental error of its ways before making a sensible return to steam and British rule.'

He seemed very pleased with himself and raised his teacup as if in toast to his plan.

Bea openly sighed before speaking. He was absolutely bonkers, but she was determined to be polite about it.

'Your plan couldn't be more wrong.'

'You're right,' he said with a smile. 'Nothing can be more wrong, as wrong is a defining feature of something not being right, and hence there is nothing that can be wronger than wrong.' He looked pleased with himself on this little lesson in English before his mind clearly saw the fundaments of the initial statement. 'But why do you believe it is wrong at all?'

'Because ...' said Bea, trying her hardest to look superior despite the restraints, '... war has always been a catalyst for advancement in technology. History has never fallen back on old ways during war but has always moved forward. The war you're creating will be the death of steam and the start of the age of diesel, or maybe even something more advanced. I'm afraid you need to stop what you're doing before you crush your own dream.'

The statement came out something like a slap, and straight away, Bea could see in the face of the doctor that what she had said had touched something inside him.

'My God, the girl's right,' he exclaimed. 'We're bringing about the end of steam by starting a war. Why didn't I see that?' He stood and looked at Beatrix with thankful compassion. 'I was making such a mistake. Civilization moves on from war; it moves back only after catastrophe.'

He turned to Igor. 'We have work to do. We need to crush every city on the Earth to the ground! We need to start all over again with a blank canvas. A brave new world that will return us back to the monkeys if we have to. We must head for Hawaii!'

He turned back to a horrified Beatrix. 'If you hadn't had come to me, I might never have noticed. The world and I are in your debt.'

He gave a deep bow, and swept from the room, Igor following behind. The mermaid looked back at Bea and gave her a hard smile as she left.

Alone in the study, Beatrix felt emotion welling up within her. A tear crept from her eye and ran down her cheek. This was hopeless. But that was not the NANI way. Beatrix sniffed and composed herself. Now, how was she going to get out of this one?

13
HELPING HANDS

'Is he dead?'

The voice came from a long way off and sounded muffled, but it was enough to make Iron open his eyes. Crouched above him was a man with a heavily-weathered face and musketeer-like facial hair, an old burn puckered his left cheek adding an untold history. The figure turned his head slightly to talk to someone out of view. Iron noted that he had a fairly common but very British accent.

'No, he's alive. The frame must have protected his body and he just got pushed into the mud. He's lucky he didn't go under and suffocate.'

'I am here, I can hear you!' said Iron, a little indignant. He tried to move but found that he was partially buried in soft, sticky earth that pulled at his limbs.

'Hold on, son, let me dig you out a little,' said the weathered man, his voice softening. 'You've taken a bit of a pasting but all in a good cause.'

The man started to dig with his hands and Iron felt

the ground relinquish its grip. He tried to stand but found something else was hampering his movements.

'Hold still. This frame is buckled; it's going to work against you. If you keep moving, you'll pop a joint.'

With some concentrated unstrapping, the stranger released most of the frame from around Iron's body and helped the boy to his feet. Iron stretched and tested his limbs. Nothing seemed broken. He turned to the man to thank him, but his words were halted as he realised that the man had a gun held to his ribs.

'Now, son, I'm only going to ask you this once, and if I don't like the answer you're going to wish you'd been left in the mud. Do you understand?'

Iron was aching too much to complain and his head felt like it had been stuffed full of cotton wool.

'So the question is: where did you get the gear?'

The gunman gestured at the helmet and frame with his gun barrel before returning it to point at Iron. Iron was crestfallen at his defeat, so just gave in on secrecy.

'I'm Iron … I mean, I'm Lord Branding and the suit is from my organisation: The Royal Order of Dragons. We hunt monsters so you don't have to.'

The man listened and then snorted with controlled laughter.

'The Royal Order of Dragons is full of old men in tweed suits, and they certainly don't give out gadgetry like this. If you are a Dragon, then why isn't there a dragon motif on your equipment? You seem to have just the head of Athena.' He tapped the maker's mark that Iron had noticed on unpacking the suit.

'It might not be Athena. It might be Britannia,' said Iron with a level of defiance. He was getting rather annoyed at the gun being pointed at him.

'Oh it's definitely Athena, the Goddess of wisdom and heroes, because it's exactly the same as mine.'

The man tapped an embroidered badge sewn onto his uniform. Indeed, the image was identical.

Iron looked at the badge for a while and said all he could think to say: 'I didn't steal it. The hotel told me it was mine.'

'It's okay, son, we're fully aware of what the hotel did. That's where we started our trail, the moment our frame went missing.'

The first voice that Iron had heard on waking spoke again, and this time his English was superb.

'Is he wearing our suit? Is he the boy?'

'Yes, sir. He is. But the suit is very beat up. I think we need to get him under cover and somehow remove it, before it fires a piston and rips his arm off.'

This last comment made Iron wince, and he happily let the gunman lead him over to another man, who appeared a lot older and better dressed.

'Of course it's never truly been tested, so you have put it through its paces. How did you find its handling?' asked the elder man as the man with the gun undid the straps and removed the helmet.

Iron breathed heavily, taking in gulps of cool fresh air. He was muddy, cold and wet and felt like he had been wearing the helmet for weeks. As it was now tucked under the man's arm, Iron could see how warped it was from the damage of the last fight.

'It handles fine. So easy to use and you feel stronger in it,' he muttered.

'Good, my boy! That's such perfect news.'

'Except … it ran out of fuel without warning and I certainly needed more ammunition for the wrist weapon.'

'It's not a weapon; it simply removes barriers.' Already the older man was opening up the ball bearing gun's empty case.

The man with the whiskers looked at the wrist gadget. 'In my experience, all weapons are for removing barriers,' he said derisively.

The other man tinkered with the gadget and the barrels flexed out slightly. 'With good practice this thing will open up corridors through anything. You had it set on the smallest aperture; you could have lost a thumb,' he told Iron with a grin, casting a sideways look at the other man, whose weapon remark had not fallen on deaf ears.

'You see,' he continued, 'this equipment belongs to us and wasn't a gift from your Society of Dragons. I'm afraid it wasn't designed to be used as a weapon; it was designed to save people.'

He held out his hand to Iron. 'Rudolph Diesel. At your service. And this gentleman is my security man.'

Iron took Diesel's hand and shook it.

'I think that's what he was doing,' interrupted the bodyguard, pointing at the footprints that led away from the village. 'Seems that by accident you've found your perfect operator.'

Both men looked at the slumping, mud-covered figure of Iron and smiled at him.

'We best get him cleaned up then.'

Iron let the men lead him over to what he had assumed was a barn. On approaching, he realised it was actually some sort of vehicle. It was as long as a train carriage but twice as tall and three times as wide. The whole thing was covered in overlapping metal plates and sloped gradually toward the rear. In fact the vehicle didn't have a single straight surface or corner; it was so contoured it looked more organic than man-made. As they came up to it, a section in the sloped rear rose and they walked inside.

The interior was configured like a well-appointed government building. Corridors and doors were decorated as if this was a static construction, but certain elements gave its mobile capabilities away. All the furniture and normal moveable objects were bolted down and every chair featured a belt to hold the occupant safely in.

The corridor opened up at the end into a large room with four smaller machines inside, each with canopy open to reveal a single driver's seat inside. The vehicles all looked like crouched sentinels, as they were supported on two mechanical legs rather than on wheels and had arm-like limbs extending from the front.

Iron was sat down in a spare chair, and Diesel wheeled a mechanic's table over and proceeded to remove with a selection of specialised tools the twisted frame still wrapped around the boy's body. The bodyguard then took the freed hero to another room, which contained a bath.

'I think your suit is a bit tattered, so while you wash I'll look you out one of my uniforms. We're about the same size.'

Iron watched the man go before running a bath for himself and taking off the tweed suit that quite clearly hadn't been designed for fighting giant monkey bears.

As he slipped into the hot water, it seemed a long time since breakfast in the Berlin hotel, and though he was glad to relax, he could certainly do with a nice meal.

After he had emerged from the water, dried himself off and dressed in the spare uniform, he was taken to another room, wherein a buffet lunch had been laid out.

As he munched on a sandwich, he found himself admiring his new outfit. He liked the dark trousers with a distinctive red stripe up the outside seam. The jacket was well-fitted and of a uniform style that had fallen from favour about 15 years earlier. It had a high straight collar and a removable panel at the front, allowing an officer to attend the field and get mucky from battle, yet to exchange the panel for a clean one if suddenly requested to appear before a superior. The most surprising thing was that the jacket had a regimental patch that was quite clearly of a dragon.

If Iron was to take a guess, it would be that this was the Royal Order of Dragons' original symbol.

As he ate, he didn't once take his eyes off the security guard, wishing so much that he knew the faces of the Order's history better. Rudolph Diesel had not joined them for food but now entered the room pulling an upright cart with a refurbished frame on it.

'It seems you might have done more good with one of these than I could ever have envisioned.'

Diesel stood the cart beside Iron and sat down.

'I've increased the fuel tank capacity on the flight pack, so you shouldn't run out as fast, but when you do: it's a simple diesel engine, so just top it up with fuel. The path-clearer is easy to reload. You just need metal ball bearings of the right size that are affected by magnetic forces. I doubt you'll ever see us again, so it might be a good idea to learn how to fix and look after it yourself. We will drop you off when you have finished eating and then you'll be on your own. I think we have all agreed that you'll use the frame wisely.'

Diesel picked up and thickly buttered a roll, while Iron lifted the frame off the cart and slid it back on over his shoulders.

Iron said nothing, as he didn't really know what to say. He had no idea who the men were, or what their plans might be. He just knew he had been handed a gift and he really wanted to keep it.

As he moved back into the large room, he was left alone with just the bodyguard.

'I'm guessing you're going back after the monster,' the man said with little emotion. 'Let me give you a word of advice from an old soldier. Always take someone to watch your back, son, however unlikely that companion may be.'

He opened up a side door in the vehicle and sunlight flooded into the room. 'You don't want to be wasting that flight pack's fuel, and Alexander Palace is a long way: you'd best take one of these.'

He gestured to the legged machines, crouching in the hold of the vehicle. Iron's eyes widened. His day had just got better.

As the giant vehicle drove off, with the distinctive splutter of large diesel engines, Iron sat watching it go. He was in the driving seat of one of the sentinel-like walkers. It was about ten foot tall and consisted of a cab supported on powerful hydraulic legs. The mechanical arms hung down, attached either side where doors would normally be. The driver sat in the cab, and an armoured cover closed down over him, protecting him as the device moved. Iron took hold of the joystick controls and, with a roar of motors and a belch of smoke, turned toward Saint Petersburg and Alexander Palace. After a few minutes, Iron had the hang of it, and made the vehicle run like an Olympic sprinter. With its great strides it easily handled terrain no wheels ever could, and Iron knew that the journey to St Petersburg would be over in a flash.

The Palace at Alexander was imposing and, with all that was going on, quite rightly heavily guarded. Iron had left his walker hidden in the trees outside the grounds and gained access through one of the upstairs windows. He had a very good idea of the layout of the servants' quarters, having grown up somewhere similar, and tapped politely on a room he knew must belong to the house nanny – the woman he had met while battling the monsters.

He had taken off his helmet and straightened his hair while waiting for Beatrix Honey to answer. He was a little taken aback when the busty form of Nana Coster opened the door instead.

'Yes?' she asked, with the voice of one who had thought her day was over.

'Erm! I ... I'm looking for Nanny Honey,' he stammered.

Nana looked him up and down and smiled. 'Well I'm sure she'll be more than happy to see you, young man, but don't you think it's a bit late to be calling on a young lady?'

He tried to put some authority back in his voice. 'It's not like that; it's about national security.'

'Well in that case, she left this morning to track down the source of the attacks. Apparently she had a lift to get her there.'

There was a long silence, and Iron and Nana looked at each other, before Nana raised her eyebrows and smiled. 'Right, I'll be saying goodnight then.' And with that she slowly shut the door.

Without the girl he had taken a huge detour to collect, and hopefully impress, Iron made his way back to the walker. He had to think. How would he find out where the base of operation was? He needed to trace the monsters back to their source and the only way he could do that was by confronting one of them.

The fact was that he had absolutely no idea where Rasputin had gone, and without the young nanny, no way of finding out. So that left him with only one remaining option. The other beast. And the last encounter really hadn't gone Iron's way.

14
LAKE FISHING

The lake was huge and tranquil.

Iron stood on the shore in his walking machine and studied the surface of the water carefully. No matter how closely he looked, he could see no sign of the creature, but he knew it would be lurking somewhere. He reasoned that whatever had turned Rasputin into a monster had left his body along with his blood. So the blood was the key here.

It seemed that the best path would be to slowly injure the remaining beast until its wounds purged it of enough blood to transform it back to its original form once more. Iron was at a loss as to what could possibly be hidden beneath the huge body of the monster, but whatever it was, he felt it could either be pressured into giving away its base of origin or else be made to flee back there as the only place of security. Either way, Iron would then have a destination to head for. The big task now was to find and fight the monster again.

It was time to flush it out. Iron had secured a box of explosives from some nearby mining operations, and it was now resting beside the walker. He popped the lid with one of the huge mechanical arms and uncovered the sticks of dynamite inside.

It was amazing how delicate the giant hands could be. He lifted a single stick of explosive from the box and, with the pilot light from the other arm's blowtorch, lit the fuse and threw the object into the lake.

The thing about giant mechanical arms is that they can throw a long way. The stick disappeared below the water and then there was a second of nothing, before a huge explosion of water and sound erupted above the surface.

Iron lit another and threw it slightly to the left. There was another funnel of water followed by the shockwave of noise. Subsequent explosions made the water erupt again and again. Iron had chosen to work his way toward a small island in the lake, setting explosions every hundred yards or so along the way.

He wasn't the best of throwers, but then it wasn't too difficult to hit a lake. He looked at the island and thought it might be interesting to try to hit it, but the first throw toward the small piece of land found the water to one side instead. Iron frowned and readjusted his aim. The next stick of dynamite landed amongst the darkened grass. There was a loud bang and a flash as the thing exploded, but then Iron gasped in surprise as the island itself stood up, water cascading off the knotted muscles of the bearboon.

The roar that filled the air was even louder than the explosion. The beast, eyes blinking from the water, turned toward the bank and saw the walker, the only object for miles. It thundered through the water, a huge white-crested wake forming before its chest as the charge grew in pace and a distinctive V of ripples spreading out behind it as it came.

Iron readied himself. This time he wasn't going to be the victim. As the creature crested the bank at the edge of the lake, it discovered that Iron had found a place of strategic importance. The shoreline suddenly rose up, and the walker was stood on deceptively higher ground. For a second the cockpit was level with the creature's head. Iron swung one of the massive mechanical arms and connected with the beast's jaw.

The bearboon spun sideways. Since taking on this monstrous body, the creature called Gruber had known very little fear. Even when faced by his brother's creation, the colossal Moscow mule, he had not felt afraid, but now, for some reason, his nerves started to show. He searched his mind for the calming voice of Dr Tripps but it was no longer there. He was alone, and the pack instinct inside him felt the isolation. The only option was to run.

As the creature scrambled for the water, Iron grabbed his leg and pulled him back onto the bank and moved to cut off his escape route. Gruber kicked out with his free foot and connected with the metal walker. Although this pushed him free of the grip and sent the vehicle spinning backwards, it also hurt the sensitive paws of the giant beast, still sore from the attack on Moscow.

Instead of pressing forward with an attack, the Berlin bear dragged itself up and struck out with a clenched fist.

Inside the walker, Iron was thrown about by the impact, prompting him to buckle his seatbelt. He raised up one of the walker's hands and caught the next blow from the creature by the wrist and held it tight. The bearboon tried to shake free. It had an advantage of height, and so lifted the machine several times and brought it crashing down onto the ground, the impact hurting the beast as much as it dented the machine.

The entire time, Iron used the walker's free hand to punch into the creature, each blow opening up cuts on the hide and bringing forth tainted blood to run down and pool on the ground. He was making sure that none of his attacks did enough damage to kill; a fact of which the bearboon was quick to take advantage.

Gruber seized the walker in both hands and raised it above his head, then brought it smashing to the ground with all the force it could muster. One leg tore off with a shower of sparks, and the hand gripping his wrist was rent from the vehicle. The cabin filled with thick smoke as the diesel engine ruptured.

Now free of the walker, the Berlin bear started to run back inland. Iron popped open the vehicle's canopy and with one flicked switch on his control pad was airborne, shooting free of the dark cloud of smoke and giving chase. He knew what Diesel had said about the wrist-mounted path-clearer not being a weapon, but he opened fire all the same.

Gruber let out a howl as the steel projectiles thudded hard into his flesh. He took two paces and fell forward. His fur was matted with blood but his chest was still rising and falling. The blood-loss was working, and the creature started to shrink in size. As Iron landed, in the grass before him was the body of a large winged baboon.

He watched it stir, testing its wings as if remembering that they were a part of its body. It stretched and coughed a few hacking breaths before looking back to the smoking, broken wreck of the walker. Seemingly happy with the destruction of its opponent and not noticing the small armoured man standing watching, it took a couple of faltering steps before rising, unsteadily, into the air.

Iron waited until the flying figure was just a speck in the sky, and then he also took to the air and followed at a discreet distance. They were quickly high above the rolling waves of the Baltic and flying toward Europe.

Iron looked down at the scenery beneath him, the helmet allowing a degree of magnification. Europe was preparing for war. He could see convoys of troops moving from Russia along the grand roads, and trains with flat bed carriages weighed down by large guns and guarded by fidgety soldiers.

The fields of Germany were being set up with rows of tents, and large flat spaces were being lined with the biplanes of the nation's social elite. The clouds above towns were becoming darker as the factories of industry stoked their furnaces to build more machines of war or to forge munitions.

They next flew over France, and Iron saw that the troops were set up in neatly-ordered battalions trained for the fighting to come. Then the sea and the ships from English dockyards covered the waves, their mix of steam and diesel clouds colouring the air. As they left European waters, everything started to calm down. Iron could feel a lump form in his throat and he wanted to go back, the desire building in his heart to help the war effort, but still the black shape in front of him drew him on. He had no idea if finding the source of the monsters would stop the war and he didn't know if Beatrix would even be there. He couldn't imagine how she could have reached it even if she was.

Finally, after many hours of following a flying baboon that appeared to have misplaced its roost, a larger shape appeared in the sky. A balloon of great size with a large, ship-like gondola suspended beneath. It was moving under its own propulsion and was certainly the destination of the flying baboon. It was moving quickly but its size made it slower than the two flying individuals.

Iron watched from a distance as the baboon landed on the ship. Then, after a few minutes, he too began his approach.

15
RESCUE

Inside the *Arc*, Dr Tripps and his beautiful assistant Igor were surrounded by plans for further Kaiju. Every blackboard was filled with exotic designs, and additional paperwork lined the walls with images of many exotic and horrifying beasts.

A giant tortoise creature with a shell made of overlapping metal plates and bristling with gun barrels was pictured beside a titanic elephant with skin made from a constantly-running slime and prehensile hands where its feet should be. A large sheet of yellowing paper featured simple designs for a salamander with more eyes than a spider, an octopus with the shell of a snail and a mountain gorilla that had more in common with a crested lizard, making it the stuff of nightmares.

Igor looked for wall space and, on finding none, placed on the back of the door a sketch of a whale covered in huge rear-facing spikes the size of tusks. As she turned, the door opened and in stumbled the panting form of Gruber. The baboon's face was slick with sweat as if it had been through the most strenuous of exercise.

Igor placed her hand on the beast's shoulder and held it still, waiting for the doctor to finish a design on the board. He seemed pleased with a beast that looked like the Chinese dragons of old, all curling, snake-like body, but with a monkey-like horned head.

As the doctor stood back to admire his handiwork, Igor coughed, and he turned, smiling.

His expression changed to a frown on seeing the winged, bedraggled creature.

'What has happened? You should be a great bear, a symbol of Germany's might and threat to the Russian people. Did I not tell you to stay hidden in the water? You wouldn't have drowned. I gave you all the abilities to survive when I created you.' He looked angry.

The baboon merely shrugged. It had no idea what was being said, it could just feel the anger. It certainly had no thoughts on why it had stopped being the creature; it just knew it had reverted back to this form after the fight. In all honesty it was just happy still to be alive.

Igor slipped a familiar crown over Gruber's head and his body went rigid as the doctor's brain-dome glowed and pulsed. Once in the creature's mind, Tripps moved through its memory like a book. Reliving the fight with the strange flying man they had crushed for his impudence. Spooling quickly through the meals of fish and beef. Then there it was: the war machine.

It was everything he knew he would hate about diesel. It belched black, choking smoke and taunted the gentle curling clouds of steam. The piston-driven limbs were harsh, mocking life, and had none of the grace of his organically-grown monsters. He replayed the fight in slow motion as his creature beat the machine back and tore it apart; but then, badly wounded, the bearboon fell and the last of the cocktail left it.

Tripps' head stopped glowing and he hooked the crown off the ape, passing it back to Igor.

'They can bleed out.'

He turned to a blackboard full of equations and snatched up a board rubber. After a moment's consideration, he rubbed off one number and wrote a letter in its place.

'There we go, now it's permanent.'

He walked past the baboon, ruffling its hair. 'Good work, Gruber. We should think about getting you a medal.'

Outside one of the portholes, Iron had listened to the whole conversation and studied the pictures and the plans to destroy the world. He knew he had to stop them but suddenly felt very alone.

Moving down the netting, he cursed letting the baboon go. The world had possibly lost its only advantage. He tried another porthole, which was shut tight, before spying a large wooden door, clearly designed for loading the craft with supplies.

As with most of these doors, it could be unbolted from the outside, so as quietly as possible, Iron let himself in. As he closed the door behind him, the rush of high-altitude air was silenced and he found himself standing amongst packing crates and the mixed, musty smells of a storeroom.

As he tiptoed between the crates, he strained his ears, listening for the slightest of movement, or a sign that he'd been discovered. He had no idea how he was intending to stop the plans he had overheard or forestall the war before it began.

He heard a tapping noise and paused, listening hard, working out where it was coming from and if it was a threat. The crates in front of him acted as a wall and the noise came from behind. So he slowly leant around to see what was on the other side.

In a cleared space was a small winged monkey sat on a box facing away from him, with a trident in its hand. Its other hand was scratching its bottom, and the wooden crate was being repeatedly tapped by the monkey's knuckles. The trident it held was pointed toward a chair, where sat a manacled woman with a small hessian sack over her head.

Iron's heart beat faster. He recognised the purple dress. Swiftly he checked that the area was clear of other creatures, then he ran up behind the monkey, matching his foot falls to the thumping scratch,. With one tap to the head with his gauntlet, the monkey was knocked out. The trident fell, but Iron caught it swiftly on the toe of his boot and lowered it to the floor.

He grasped the sack and pulled it off, revealing the gagged and blinking face of Beatrix Honey.

He held a finger to the mouth of his helmet to indicate quiet. Bea rolled her eyes and gave him an angry look, which was as easy to read: 'I'm gagged! What noises do you think I'd be making?'

He turned back to the monkey and scooped it up in the sack, undid Bea's gag and used it to tie the sack closed.

'Hello,' Bea whispered, more than pleased to see her flying knight again. 'You need to get me out of here quickly; there's a maniac on board. He plans to destroy the world.'

'I know. I just overheard him. I don't think I've helped; I may have unintentionally let him know his only weakness.'

Bea looked sympathetic but chose not to explain

how she had inadvertently convinced Tripps to destroy the world completely rather than rely on war.

Iron tried the manacles around the girl's hands, which were securely locked. He looked around but could see no obvious key. 'Do you have a hair pin I could borrow, to pick these locks?'

'Yes definitely, but you'll have to get it yourself.'

So Iron lent in and gently rummaged through Bea's hair, taking out a couple of clips and letting her tresses fall down. Her hair was longer than he had expected, and was soft to the touch.

'What?' said Bea, when she realised that the helmeted man was not moving.

'Nothing, just thinking,' said Iron, glad of the helmet that hid his blushes, aware he'd been simply staring at the beautiful girl before him. He bent down by the lock, hair pin in hand.

'I'm very impressed you can pick locks,' she said, trying not to show too much admiration. It was at this precise moment that Iron realised he couldn't pick locks and never had. However, he was about to give it his best British try.

It was a good few minutes later that Iron uttered the following lie: 'Dashed clever, that. The fellow's used reversed tumblers. I'll have to lever them open.'

Hoping his inability hadn't been spotted, he picked up the monkey's trident and using the lever principle forced the locks apart.

He had released both of Bea's hands, her waist and forehead before the trident broke. There was an embarrassing moment for both Bea and Iron as he knelt down before her and tried to use the strength of the frame to pull the ankle manacles free. The strain was quite taxing and the helmet was getting Iron hot, so he slipped it off to try again.

There was a gasp from Bea.

'What?' This time it was Iron who was concerned, and unfortunately for Beatrix she had no helmet to hide her blush, so just had to bluster through.

'You're quite young for a Lord ...' she said.

Iron was suddenly aware this was the first time she had seen his face, and he too blushed, remembering the deception of his identity.

'Er, yes, my, er, father passed away when I was young. I inherited his estate. My friends call me Iron.'

He hated the lie, but it was for the protection of his benefactor more than anything. Wanting to distract them both, he pulled as hard as he could and broke the final bonds, freeing the nanny. She jumped up, quickly adjusting her skirts.

Bea set about grabbing the pile of her things as Iron replaced his helmet.

'We need to get out of here and to solid ground, where we can plan, safely,' she said. 'Can you carry us both?'

'I've never really needed to try, but the flight pack is pretty powerful.'

The two of them walked to the door and Iron pulled it open carefully. The sudden rush of air and noise filled the storeroom. He wrapped his arm around Bea's waist and she placed hers around his neck and they launched themselves into the air.

Free of the ship, Iron looked toward the ground, but the cloud was heavy and any breaks showed only blue sea far below.

It was Bea who looked back to the ship, so she saw it first. The *Arc* was docking on a huge platform in the sky, with buildings and streets, all styled in the architecture of a Victorian industrial town. The clouds around it were so heavy that it appeared to be part of them. Although they were some distance away, the streets could be seen to have figures moving upon them. Some were moving toward the dock, ready to accept Dr Tripps' return, no doubt, and to try and carry out his plans against humanity and the world.

16
STEAM CITY

The Steam City in the clouds was like something from a dream. Its buildings were squat like those of the dockyards of Great Britain but there was only one port, which was where the majestic *Arc* would moor when the doctor was at home. The buildings lined a large, cobbled square. Workshops with squat chimneys ranged along one side while living accommodation lined the other. Every house had its own garden, dedicated to vegetable patches and herbs. Located behind all the houses were pens full of varied livestock that added a fragrance all of their own to the air.

The streets at first appeared to be occupied by typical residents, but on closer inspection it could be clearly seen they were a melting pot of different primates, all dressed in clothes befitting their occupations. Amongst them was also the occasional experimental hybrid; a horse-man pulling a handcart or a creature more nightmare than mammal.

In fact humans were in the minority. They were there, but they clearly weren't residents but instead agents from the surface, who could blend in easier there than their more incongruous collaborators. The human agents were all wearing prominent badges on their lapels, depicting winged skulls complete with moustaches, as if without them the nonhuman residents would revolt and throw them from the platform.

At the far end of the square was a replica of the glass laboratory and home that Tripps had left back on the destroyed Limehouse docks. It squatted like a great glass-and-metal turtle that had dragged itself to shore, and it was to this building that Tripps and his entourage now travelled. They walked past four glass domes in the square with round escape hatches beside them. All but one of these domes contained the rounded top of a colourful balloon, and it was suddenly apparent how the steamer agents could get from the ground to the city and back so easily.

Tripps entered his home, followed by Igor and Flyn. The two baboons waited by the door, a huge travelling chest held between them. Igor waved them inside as the doctor was already heading into his laboratory.

The baboons entered and the chest was opened. So many bottles of different coloured cocktails filled the box that when the sun hit it the room, they shone like a rainbow. Even outside, the occupants of the city were distracted from their work as the windows of the Tripps Mansion glowed with colour.

Hidden in the clouds outside the city, Iron and Bea hovered looking for a place to land safely. Any thoughts of landing on the ground beneath the city had left them the moment they broke through the clouds and found themselves above the very active volcanic chain of Hawaii. Now they were back by the platform and looking to land on enemy ground. The only place they could find was the animal pens. There was a ledge where the enclosures didn't run right up to the edge of the platform, and the enclosed backs would give them a degree of cover from any watching eyes.

It was a bit of precision-flying that Iron wasn't very confident about undertaking. He flew past first and checked out the best place to set down, and then moved in. Unfortunately he hadn't fully allowed for the additional weight of carrying Bea, and the two of them hit the back of the animal pens quite hard and made a fair bit of noise.

The pair of intruders stood stock still, listening to the panicked sounds of the cattle within. Suddenly, a door popped open. Neither of them had noticed any doors here when hovering, as they had thought there was no reason for anyone to come out on this side of the platform.

The figure that walked out onto the ledge was shocking in appearance. Resembling a diminutive metal man, it was about four feet tall and rotund in design, with comical legs and long arms. The body's designer had most certainly been influenced by chimpanzees. At the shoulders, though, the chimpanzee element stopped, and where the head should have been there was a sunken cockpit surrounded by buttons, in the middle of which sat a rabbit.

'At. Last!' said a very British voice. 'Took. A. Fair. Few. Days. For. The. Agency. To. Send. Someone. And. I. See. They. Gave. You. A. Chauffer.' The rabbit was eagerly pressing buttons to form speech, which then emerged from a grille on the front of the robot.

Bea was understandably surprised and speechless and looked from the rabbit to Iron and then back. She composed herself. After all, a nanny should be able to deal with every eventuality.

'I'm sorry, but you have me at a loss. Should I know you?' she asked, as politely as she could, causing the rabbit to press buttons at a furious rate.

'I. Am. Harry. Ma'am. I. Am. The. Operator. Who. Sent. The. Message. To. NANI. Informing. Of. The. Threat. To. The. Romanov. Children. I. Assume. You. Have. Traced. The. Threat. Back. Here. And. Have. Come. To. Nip. It. In. The. Bud.'

The voice stopped and the rabbit stood to attention. Iron didn't know what to do, and so simply saluted. Bea could only smile, and was particularly impressed at the young Lord not becoming upset by being reduced to the level of below-stairs staff by a talking rabbit.

'Well, we've certainly taken the long route round, but we're here now,' she said with a disarming grin.

'Come. Inside. We. Have. Much. To. Talk. About. The. Doctor. Has. Returned. And. I. Fear. The. Worst.'

With that, the rabbit-controlled robot disappeared back through the door, to be followed by the nanny and the counterfeit Lord.

Harry the rabbit was the perfect host, with a house of his own on the platform. It transpired he came from a long line of lepus agents: many of whom, favouring a mistress over a master, had found themselves falling into the employ of NANI. It was in this capacity that Harry had become embroiled with the work of Dr Tripps. Over the past couple of years he had observed its every detail, but when the doctor's plans had threatened to become harmful to the children under the protection of NANI, he had raised the alarm. He had expected someone to come, and therefore he had a plan all ready.

So, with a pot of Earl Grey tea, a selection of cakes and lashings of ginger beer, the strange trio sat around a kitchen table, discussing the best way to take down the most important criminal mastermind since Moriarty.

'The. Whole. Platform. Is. Kept. Aloft. By. A. Solution. Painted. Onto. Its. Underside. Created. By. A. Friend. Of. The. Doctor's. It. Completely. Negates. The. Effects. Of. Gravity. On. Any. Surface.' Harry said, and Bea thought she could detect an air of admiration in the electronic voice.

'Why doesn't it just fly out into space?' Iron asked. He had removed his helmet earlier, so he felt the full force of the rabbit's gaze, but could see on Bea's face she had wanted to ask the same question

'It's simple physics,' he continued. 'Gravity is the only thing that keeps us here. Without it, we'd simply fly away.'

Harry took a nibble of carrot cake before answering.

'The. Solution. Is. Made. With. Extreme. Heat. The. Gravity. Defying. Properties. Happen. After. It. Cools. Only. As. You. Said. No. Gravity. And. You're. Spaceward. Bound.'

Iron allowed himself a happy smile, and he believed Bea actually gave him a wink.

'The. Reason. The. Doctor. Built. The. Platform. Above. The. Volcanoes. Is. The. Warm. Air. It. Keeps. The. Solution. From. Fully. Cooling. So. We'll. Only. Partially. Avoid. Gravity. The. Whole. Platform. Is. At. The. Optimum. Height. Any. Lower. And. The. Heat. Would. Melt. The. Solution. And. We'd. Crash. Into. The. Ground. Any. Higher. And. We'd. Cool. With. A. One.

Way. Ticket. To. Space.

'Despite. All. That. Tripps. Always. Stays. At. Home. There. Is. An. Upper. Storey. But. You. Can. Bet. They. Will. All. Be. In. The. Laboratory. There. Are. Two. Ways. In. One. Is. Through. The. Front. Door. Which. Will. Ring. A. Bell. And. Fetch. Either. Igor. Or. Flyn. His. Butler. Instantly. The. Other. Is. Through. The. Skylights. Which. Will. Mean. You. Have. All. Of. Them. At. Once. But. Will. Have. The. Element. Of. Surprise.'

'I think I met this Flyn,' Bea said.

'You'd. Know. If. You. Did. Tripps. Created. The. Loyal. Little. Gremlin. Many. Years. Ago. Using. A. Teleportation. Machine. Seems. If. Two. Things. Got. Into. The. Machine. They. Would. Blend. Together. Luckily. The. First. Thing. Through. Was. His. Monkey. Butler. Rather. Than. A. Human. The. Thing. Is. He. Is. Still. Loyal. He. Just. Has. A. Lot. Of. Fly. In. Him. Clouds. His. Judgement. Sometimes. But. Makes. Him. Deceptively. Agile.'

Iron sat back in his chair and looked at the plans for a long time. Then he walked to the window and looked toward the *Arc* tethered at the port, before turning back to the room.

'Is there an evacuation plan?' he asked.

'Of. Course.'

'Right. Harry, give us five minutes, then start an evacuation.'

Iron pulled his helmet on and motioned for Bea to follow him. As he walked toward the back door, he grabbed a big jar of strawberry jam from beside Harry's home-cooked scones. 'Do you mind if I take this?'

Harry smiled a big rabbitty smile.

'It. Would. Be. My. Pleasure.'

They walked back through the well-appointed

garden and into the cowshed, avoiding any watchful eyes.

'I hope you can use that thing?' Iron said, pointing at Bea's umbrella. 'It might be useful …'

Harry watched as the couple took off from behind the cowshed and vanished into the sky.

17
PEOPLE IN GLASS HOUSES

Igor and Flyn stacked the last of the multicoloured bottles while Tripps moved small figures of monsters around on his world map. Chuckling to himself, the doctor swapped two figures over, grew silent, then began to chuckle louder.

A claxon sound penetrated the air and everyone looked up from what they were doing.

It was an evacuation.

Just under the sound of the alarm there was a rushing noise like rockets. The glass windows above them shattered and the airborne figure of Iron streaked into the room.

His jets blew bottles from shelves and paperwork from desks as he landed in the centre, a cloud of detritus blowing and settling around him.

Tripps' brain-case bubbled in anger, and he practically screamed: '*Get him!*'

With the agility of a chimpanzee and the erratic

movements of a fly, the hybrid Flyn soared across the room, grabbing a metal test tube holder as he went. The strong stem became a handle and the weighted base looked lethal. Reaching down, Iron pulled the pot of jam from his pocket and threw it at the window. It hit the glass, cracking the pane but shattering the jar in a splash of sticky, sweet strawberry preserve.

Flyn barrelled straight past Iron toward the jam, his little wings buzzing in the most delighted way. He hit the window at full pelt and the broken pane gave way. The happy flybrid plunged through the clouds, all thoughts of impending oblivion obscured by the sweet, rich, sticky goodness that he was stuffing into his insectile mouth parts with his simian hands.

The howl of despair that came from Tripps' mouth as his loyal butler disappeared was heartfelt. The smile that crossed Igor's face was also evident; right up to the point when Bea drifted through an open skylight on her umbrella

Responding to the doctor's shouts, the two baboons, Peter and Gruber, came flying into the room, fangs bared, not sure what was going on but confident it was a call to arms. The first thing Peter saw was Bea, his Alpha female, who merely lifted an eyebrow and positioned her feet firmly on the floor. Beside him, Gruber continued his charge. Peter realised that to protect his Alpha, he had to take his brother down.

Gruber was surprised when Peter pounced on him and forced him to the ground. The two apes rolled in a big ball of snarling rage across the floor, disappearing amongst the foliage, to which all eyes turned, especially the disbelieving ones of Tripps and Igor.

Snapping her umbrella closed, Bea lifted the point to aim at the unarmed Igor's throat.

'Don't even think about leaping, lassie. I'd fillet you as you flew.'

Iron pointed his wrist-mounted weapon at Tripps and smiled beneath the helmet.

'I do love it when the good guys win, don't you, Professor?'

Dr Tripps scowled. 'I think you'll find good guys only win because they're the ones who write the history books. And I'm a doctor, not a professor.'

'Well I doubt we'll be seeing your name in any books. What exactly are you a doctor of, anyway?'

Tripps smiled. 'Amongst so many other things, I majored in botany.' With a flash of concentration, his cranium glowed and a series of mighty green tendrils whipped from the foliage at the far side of the room, wrapping themselves around Iron and Bea and hoisting them into the air.

Bea's umbrella clattered to the floor, and she frowned as once again her skirt fell to her ears as the vegetation held her upside down. For some reason, she really hoped Iron was looking the other way.

'Well, well, well,' said Tripps, gently smoothing his moustache with his fingers. 'It appears that the good guys will indeed win again; and when we do, I shall make sure the history books remember your names as the first two Kaiju who made it all possible. Igor, fetch me two cocktails!'

Gliding and giggling, Igor selected two bottles from the shelf, uncorked them, releasing a curl of smoke from each, and held them up. Green vines stretched forward, taking the bottles from her, before moving to the two upside-down heroes.

Tripps walked forward and slipped off Iron's helmet.

'Wouldn't want to get any in your nice hat now, would we?'

Bea and Iron both clamped their lips tightly together, but a simple constriction by the tendrils forced them to open their mouths again as they gasped for breath. They struggled to escape, seemingly in vain, as the colourful liquids were slowly being brought forward.

Suddenly, Iron realised that his wrist was free, and he let rip with all that his wrist-mounted path-clearer had.

The ball bearings ripped the foliage apart and freed his arm long enough for him to point. Aiming carefully, he shot a small hole right through the wall in front of him, and kept firing until the empty barrel of the weapon just clicked.

Tripps looked first at the light streaming through his front wall and then back at Iron's upside-down face. He laughed. 'Well that was a strange display of last heroics.'

But the laugh caught in his throat as the entire platform lurched to an alarming angle, throwing him from his feet and spinning Igor back across the floor into the far wall, no matter how much she applied the brakes.

Outside, Iron's shots had gone exactly where he had wanted. He had torn apart the balloon of the *Arc*. As this was not coated with any anti-gravity solution, it had behaved as any heavy object in the sky would do. It had started to fall.

Tied so firmly to the platform, it was pulling the whole thing down at the far end.

As the end dipped, it started to warm as it came closer to the volcanoes below. Very slowly it was starting to bring the whole platform down. Like a seesaw, it had forced the end with Tripps' laboratory up higher, and that area was starting to cool. The whole city was starting to break up under the strain, tipping the platform one way then the other as opposing forces pulled on it from either end.

Igor was being spun like a top, and the sudden jolts were certainly affecting her ability to control her movements. As the doctor regained his footing, she careered straight into him and carried them both into the dark forest of his laboratory with a loud crash.

Instantly both Bea and Iron were released and dropped to the floor with a thud. Poor Iron hit a bench and was winded, but the cat-like Beatrix landed on her feet, grabbed her umbrella and was instantly by his side.

'We've got to go! The whole city is being destroyed,' she shouted above the sounds of crashing glass and rending metal.

The two ran uncertainly outside. They could see that the ringing alarms had cleared the platform of most inhabitants, except for a few stray apes who seemed to be enjoying the excitement.

Skidding and sliding, Iron and Bea reached the dock end of the platform. Just as they did, it tore away, the falling *Arc* spinning down into the bright red mouth of a volcano below. Then at a terrific rending sound behind them, they both turned in time to see the doctor's laboratory tear free and shoot at an alarming rate up into the heavens, speeding like some enormous star turtle. With both opposing forces gone, the tremors subsided. The platform bent and buckled, returned to its optimum height and stabilised.

A moment passed as Beatrix looked at Iron, classically handsome, splendid in his uniform, and Iron looked back at Beatrix, a vision with her honey-coloured hair flowing in the wind. Their eyes met, and then they both started laughing uncontrollably.

Beatrix held out her hand. 'Thank you, Lord Branding, of the Royal Order of Dragons. It does indeed appear your help *was* needed in this case.'

Iron took her hand, and, not really knowing what was expected of him, shook it firmly.

'Thank you, Nanny Honey. If the Empire is ever in danger again, I shall be sure to get them to look you up.' They both laughed again, then turned to watch the sunset over Hawaii, still holding hands …

Beatrix looked across at the knight beside her.

'Your name is Iron Branding?' she said with a smile, as if she had only just realised.

He laughed. 'You can talk! You're called Bea Honey.'

EPILOGUE

A few months later, war had erupted across Europe. It was inevitable. No-one really knew where the monsters had come from, but they all decided to lay the blame with their enemies rather than look further afield.

The soldiers of the world were not so different really. They all fought for their countries and believed the propaganda about their enemies. Most were young and had never been at war before, and nearly all were scared, especially when the night came and the talk turned to monsters.

One young soldier had come from the home counties of England. He listened to the talk of his fellow soldiers, then rolled up his kit as a pillow and lay on his back, looking up at the moon and thinking of a young nanny he once met, wondering if she was looking up at the moon too and thinking of him.

The moon, the glorious reflective orb that looked down on all below.

High above the Earth, the moon looked down. Amid its swathes of grey dust, seas and peaks was a dome that looked something like a glass-and-metal turtle.

The dome was sealed tight by some very clever airlocks, and inside were plants, fed by the carbon fumes of the mammals, replenishing the air with oxygen.

Elsewhere in the dome was a room. Decorated in a civil Edwardian style, with wooden panels, velvet drapes and lavish furniture. It was also covered in paintings and drawings, and several blackboards were standing in the corners.

Igor, her hair midnight blue and sparkling with little points of silver, set the cut crystal glass down on the table, uncorked a round dark bottle of Hendrick's finest gin and poured.

A gramophone played 'Claire de Lune' softly in the background as two figures watched the Earth rise above the horizon. The pictures of great beasts looked down from all the walls. One blackboard was covered with several rocket designs, and to another was pinned a blueprint for a big gun with liquid-filled shells.

Dr Horatio Tripps closed his eyes, sipped his gin, and smiled.

ABOUT THE AUTHOR

Kit Cox spends most of his time surrounded by monsters in his underground Victorian study. Growing up in the shadow of Chatham dockyard Kit took to drawing at the age of five and clearly could only see a world populated by big game hunters wrestling dinosaurs and girls in skimpy clothes, flying jet packs. When the pictures failed to tell the whole story he took to writing.

Kit's first and internationally nominated book, *How to Bag a Jabberwock*, written under the guise of Major Jack Union, unlocked this world to everyone. Inspired by the weirdness and wonder of real history and sprinkled with the fantastical fiction of the Edwardian era's science romance (the forerunner to Sci Fi) Kit continues to bring that world to life for a modern audience and hopefully inspire people to check out the real Historical mysteries hiding within his stories.

24300196R10082

Made in the USA
Charleston, SC
19 November 2013